W9-CHD-604

LIQUID
SKY

A novel based on the screenplay
by Slava Tsukerman, Anne Carlisle, and Nina V. Kerova

Based on the Movie *Liquid Sky*

Starring: Anne Carlisle • Paula E. Sheppard •
Bob Brady • Susan Doukas
Elaine C. Grove • Stanley Knap • Jack Adalist •
Otto Von Wernherr
Screenplay by: Slava Tsukerman • Anne Carlisle •
Nina V. Kerova
Director of Photography: Yuri Neyman
Production and Costume Design: Marina Levikova
Executive Producer: Robert Field
Associate Producer: Nina V. Kerova
Produced and Directed by Slava Tsukerman
Copyright © Z - Films, 1982

LIQUID

SKY

THE NOVEL

Anne Carlisle

A novel based on the screenplay
by Slava Tsukerman, Anne Carlisle, and Nina V. Kerova

A DOLPHIN BOOK
Doubleday
NEW YORK
1987

All of the characters in this book are fictitious, and any resemblance to actual persons, living or dead, is purely coincidental.

Library of Congress Cataloging-in-Publication Data

Carlisle, Anne, 1956–
Liquid sky.

1. Liquid sky (Motion picture)   I. Title.
PS3553.A7173L5   1987   813'.54   87–13548
ISBN 0-385-23930-0

Copyright © 1987 by Anne Carlisle
ALL RIGHTS RESERVED
PRINTED IN THE UNITED STATES OF AMERICA
FIRST EDITION

LIQUID
SKY

A novel based on the screenplay
by Slava Tsukerman, Anne Carlisle, and Nina V. Kerova

As long as she could remember, she always had the best hair. Everyone else in her family had thin, dribbly hair. But before she dropped out of college, the boys called her "that girl with the hair." It was thick and curly and there was a lot of it. Sometimes it had been overwhelming. She couldn't control it. Her mother used to say, "You're so lucky," and poke at her curls, fluffing the ringlets and sighing as though the hair wasn't attached to Margaret's head. She never knew if she was pretty or not. People said she was. She couldn't see it. But she knew her hair looked good.

Men liked it. When they were fucking her from behind she would swing it around. They liked that. Funny, how she always thought of them as they. They all seemed like one,

big, collective man. But now it was Adrian, and Adrian was
a she, not one of them.

Not that Adrian treated her so different from them. She
didn't. But when Adrian gave her the once-over, with her
approving nod, Margaret felt beautiful. With the men she
felt good. Powerful sometimes, because she knew what to
do. She lost herself in what she knew they liked. But it was
only Adrian who made her feel numb. She would get paralyzed, kind of, and not be able to think anything. And then,
if Adrian kept paying attention to her, she would feel a
warm, oozy glow all over. It was sexy. Sometimes it made
her sick to her stomach. But no matter how mean Adrian
was acting, Margaret couldn't do anything against it. It
seemed like Adrian was the only person who really saw her.

When Margaret was first with Adrian, the idea of it really
freaked her out. Especially after that redhead had come on
to her. No female had ever done that to Margaret before.
The redhead had come up to her on the street and said,
"You're hot, baby," and Margaret was sure that it showed.
People could see that she had had sex with a woman. She
had always been "artistic"; people treated her different.
Now she was a lesbian too, forever cursed. Then Margaret
thought, That's life. You've always been a freak. Now it's
out in the open. You better get used to it. Anyway, maybe
the redhead had reacted that way because of her hair. Her
new hair gave her away.

As she looked back over her life Margaret felt her past
had been one big doubt. After she did something, she
would worry; how it went, who thought what, why it turned
out the way it did, but mostly she agonized over what she
should have done. The only time she could remember being
right, feeling like she was making a real, great, move, was
when she chopped off her hair. She cried, and everyone
gave her a hard time about it, but it was worth it. It was

worth it for that one moment. She knew, at that moment, without a doubt, that she had done the right thing. After all, it was her hair. And that felt better than anything ever.

Not that she hadn't had orgasms before. But it only happened when she was on top, in the rare case when the guy would relinquish his position. It had never seemed worth upsetting the applecart for, then. Anyway they were happier if you faked it. They always said that they would hate it if a girl faked. But what's to hate if they couldn't tell the difference?

She had been every man's fantasy girl. She had been winning at the deception game. The ease of it had frightened her. That was why she cut her hair. There would be no more lies. No more faking it. She wouldn't be sorry anymore. No matter whether they liked it or not.

That's why Adrian was so mad. Because Margaret wouldn't fake it, not even for Adrian. Adrian had fucked her really hard for two days and rolled off her, exhausted. Then Margaret had climbed on top of her and had an orgasm. Adrian had yelled, "It's not true. You're a liar." Then she had tried to pull her hair. But there wasn't much of it left to pull. Anyway, that's why Adrian hated her. And everyone else was upset about her hair too. If you change something for yourself, even if they are supposed to love you, people always get you back. They punish you for it. Well, fuck it. Fuck them. Fuck you.

Club Life

They never talked among themselves. Yet they knew who was one of them. It was clear. There are some things that are beyond words. There was them, and the scabs. The scabs being the ones who tried to be like the them. There was little comfort in that. Still, no one was warm to each other within the them. If you're not nice, you're not lying. When they walked back from the Club at dawn, there was comfort only in their collective loneliness. Everyone is alone. This is not sad. Alienation is something you wear.

If you are different, you should wear it brilliantly. And they did. The style changed as they changed. The innovators could tell the imitators because they were always behind. If you couldn't tell from the clothes you could tell from the eyes. Eye bags were worn with pride. After all, you have to earn them, especially if you are young.

Adrian was the most conservative dresser. But then again, being so short and crazy, she didn't need to change her look. She always wore black, but kept her honey-colored hair long and natural, which was weird enough in her world. Margaret had never seen her touch it, but it always looked perfect. She wore this black thing low on her forehead to keep it out of her face. No makeup, but for the others, changing the face, hair, and dress was the major activity of the day. Margaret couldn't remember when they started to apply this to the house as well. Probably around the same time when in the apartment and in the Club became the same.

The apartment was full of street collectables and lit with neon signs they had stolen from a store in Harlem. Adrian had organized the heist, so no one was surprised when none of the signs worked. It was a good thing Adrian knew junkies that knew how to fix things. The only piece of furniture left from Margaret's past was a makeup mirror that she had managed to keep after all her moves. But she wasn't moving anymore. Somehow this place was it.

The best was the roof. It was bigger than the apartment itself, and right outside the back door. You could watch Manhattan for hours, sunbathe, eat out there, everything. It was particularly exciting to lean over the railing and look at the sidewalk below. The cars looked like little toys. Twenty stories above the pavement and the only living quarters in the building. The entire building was deserted after five o'clock, which was when they would get out of bed to get ready to go out. Of course, it was illegal to live there, and the building only had insurance coverage if the apartment was used as an office, nine to five. They had bribed an elevator attendant for a copy of his keys.

At night in the apartment, it almost seemed like you were in the Club. Because of all the mirrors and neon lights the whole place seemed to glitter like a dance floor in a disco. In the middle of the room, toward the windows to the roof, stood the five-foot-tall tree of broken glass. When they first started building the mirror tree, others would drop by to buy dope from Adrian, and if they weren't scabs, they would let them help glue the glass to the boughs. This was a pretty popular activity because of the blood. It was real easy to cut yourself. You could get some pretty neat scars hanging around that tree. People would drop by to cop or make a payment and never leave. They would sit in the shards of glass in a circle around the skeleton of the leafless tree, and suck each other's wounds. Margaret couldn't remember how long it took to make the tree. As time separated the users from the people seeking a social life, the group got smaller. Eventually, most got bored with the tree; the quiet ritual was too ungratifying. As with everything domestic, Margaret finished the task herself. Adrian would enter the apartment, without speaking suck the blood from Margaret's fingers, and then leave again. Margaret lost all track of time. All she knew was that her hands were healed by the time of the fashion show.

Jimmy had been even more meticulous than usual when dressing for the Club that evening. He had to model in the fashion show and needed to know he looked good. Pumping his ego was part of his toilet. He spent a good deal of time in front of the full-length mirror, examining his face, the way the clothes hung on his body, how to project the perfect look. He knew he was tall, but not too tall, slim, but not too thin; that he had good skin, offset to a dramatic advantage by his shocking bleached locks. When his slicked and wavy hair fell into his blue eyes, he knew just how to push it back, the perfect expression that went with the action. His one-sided, cynical smile was movie-star perfect. He even knew where to stand when he got to the Club, where, in each area, he could get the best light. All his preparation really paid off. His bad-boy attitude worked well with his apparently Aryan-looking genes. As he leaned on the wall at the Club (in his standing place), Jimmy's charisma was undeniable.

He knew that Adrian had to perform first. Jimmy had overheard one of the doormen discussing what Adrian's reaction might be. Of course, she would be pissed off that she was told to go on at eleven. He saw her close to eleven o'clock standing near the pillars in the back. For sure she would be in a sour mood, but still he would ask her for some stuff. He knew she probably wouldn't give him any, and it would aggravate her if he asked for it. But he was bored and didn't know what else to do with himself. And, he thought cynically, you never know about Adrian. She might give it to me. She can do anything. She's nuts.

Margaret was with Adrian. Sometimes they weren't together. Sometimes he had been hanging out with Margaret —a lot. Until everyone started saying that they looked like brother and sister. It was terrible, when people started to notice. He couldn't be associated with *her*. Anyway, anyone can look alike if they have bleached hair, Jimmy assured himself. He wondered how long it took for Margaret to bleach out her hair. It took so long for his to bleach up that he had to take downs. He didn't want to do that, they made him all slobbery. But what could he do? He had to have something against the burning. Adrian was never available during the day, and he couldn't go East to cop by himself. So he took the risk of drooling while the scab worked on his hair. Actually, the hair person he was using usually wasn't too bad. Still, you can pee on them, but you don't drool in front of them.

Jimmy figured he was brilliant. He would just flash his seductive smile at Margaret and she would think he was after her. They lived together; Adrian kept the drugs at home. So it wouldn't be too hard to get his high from her. Women always gave him drugs. It was the easiest thing to get from the scabs. The girls were easiest; all you had to do was to be consistently terrible to them and they loved you. Sometimes they gave him clothes.

A guy last month gave him a real beautiful pair of Italian shoes, brand new. Of course, he owned the shoe store. If you stayed at their house, no matter how abusive you were, sometimes they still got it up. It depended on how rich they were. He had to let him do it. I got too high and stayed there too long; now the pig comes to the Club every night and acts like he has the right to speak to me. Jimmy reviewed his mistake. I told him to fuck off a million times, but still the guy comes back for more. It was embarrassing. Funny too, though, 'cause sometimes the people Jimmy was with would tell him to fuck off too. And then they would ask the shoe guy for money! He saw him give some to Margaret the other night. It frightened him. Jimmy hoped the pig didn't tell Margaret. He didn't want anyone to know he let him do it.

Jimmy was surprised. He went right up to Adrian and said, "Hey, I need some stuff," and she asked him for money. Just like that! He hadn't believed it would work. He hadn't figured she would give him any dope, so he wasn't prepared. But he kept his cool even though he hadn't gathered any money from the scabs yet. "I'll pay you tomorrow," he said. Adrian knew he could get money from his mom. But she refused to front him the smack! So he had to use his other plan. He asked Margaret to go to her house with him. So it turned out the same as he had thought.

"Right now with you?" she had said, smiling. Jimmy

smiled back, thinking, All that coke affects her brains. But it was cool. He liked their apartment. Jimmy felt comfortable there. Especially at night it seemed a homier version of the Club, with the colored neon and funky decor. And the apartment had good light. Even a geek would look nice in the subtle clash of colored neon. Margaret put on some records as soon as they got to her place. Jimmy noticed that his clothes went well with the colors in Margaret's apartment. Good music, a cool ambiance, it was going good until the bitch started dancing. Because she was looking at him. She was moving and turning and looking at Jimmy. He couldn't get over how fast she spoiled everything. She started jumping around like a chicken, and he was supposed to find that exciting!

Adrian wondered where Margaret had gone to. She turned around to talk to someone and when she looked back, Margaret was gone. I hope that bitch doesn't fall for Jimmy Slick's cheap talk. That's what she called him in her mind. Jimmy Slick. Great name for a record. When she first met Margaret she looked like a girl from Vassar. That's what Adrian had liked about her. That, and the way she looked at him. She seemed supportive, devoted to Owen. So it was weird when Margaret let her kiss her so easy. She even seemed to like it. But what settled it for Adrian was when Margaret looked at her the same way that she had looked at Owen. Of course, Margaret had to look down to see Adrian, but it still made her feel important. Anyway, a young girl shouldn't be with an old guy like that. It was real disgusting. Even if he did know a lot.

Margaret had thought that males liked it when she danced. But it was clear that the snot Jimmy didn't. Still, she couldn't stop just 'cause he didn't like it. That would be too obvious. She couldn't believe it. He didn't look at her legs once! Not once! Maybe young ones are different, she caught herself thinking. No, stupid, Jimmy is different; he's like you. Still, she thought, I could have sworn he was looking at me "like that" before I brought him here to my place. And your corny bourgeois heart went pit-pat, Margaret admonished herself. She was overwhelmed with self-loathing. Then Jimmy put on her purple dress. He took off his jacket and slipped the dress on over his shirt. It stopped Margaret in her tracks. For a moment she had to stop dancing. He looked devastating.

Jimmy hated her. The longer she danced, the more nauseated he became. He thought she would never stop. What did she expect him to do? Sweep her off her feet like in some corny movie? Well, if she's going to be corny, I'll teach her, thought Jimmy sadistically. On the other hand, he reconsidered, I better not hurt her too bad. 'Cause suddenly, he needed to get high real bad.

"I don't usually fuck girls." There, he said it. It worked too. She stopped dancing. He needed something right away. "Do you know where she keeps the stuff?"

It was like Margaret's worst fear come true. Jimmy didn't want her; he just came after Adrian's shit. What did he take her for, a scab? If she wasn't one, why had his manipulation worked on her? She should have known. But she had fallen for his good looks and bad-boy charm as easily as any Bridge and Tunnel housewife. She had thought, We're so much alike. I could help him, I know him. We'd look great together. But he had tricked her like he would an outsider. And she had fallen for it. That was the real humiliation.

It seemed like all the lowlifes in the world were going to pass through her apartment on their way to die. She couldn't remember how she let it happen. The more rent Adrian paid, the less Margaret had to say about it. Adrian had wanted to pay for everything, just like a man. Now Margaret didn't have any normal clothes left. I'm dependent, she would think helplessly. Often Margaret tried to figure a way out of her situation. How can I go for a job interview? Anyway, what can *I* do? she thought. No one will hire me with my hair like this.

Jimmy knew that he had done it sloppily. But anyway, Margaret should understand. What was the big deal if he took a little stuff from the selfish midget's stash? Margaret went to the makeup table and started sucking on her flask. She was ignoring him! Jimmy couldn't believe it. Frustrated, he demonstratively started looking for the stash, rattling through the drawers of her makeup vanity, and checking behind its mirrors. But Margaret didn't respond, except to utter an obligatory "Cut it out." He watched her as she flopped down on the platform bed, unconsciously displaying her legs. He didn't exist! Now that he didn't want to fuck, he was a non-person. She wasn't aware of him. Margaret no longer took him seriously. It always boils down to that, thinks an enraged Jimmy. He takes the drinking glass off the makeup table and throws it at the operating record player. It shatters, stopping the music. At least the bitch won't dance anymore, he thinks, laughing to himself. Why wouldn't she give him what he needed? "You ugly old whore. You make me sick," he raged. "If you don't give me the stuff I'm going to rat on you." Immediately after it came from his mouth Jimmy knew it was ridiculous. How could he rat on Adrian and Margaret? They were his only steady and clean supply. If he turned them in he'd end up OD'd in an alley somewhere. In frustration, Jimmy reaches for the shoe rack.

The shoe rack at one time was probably a functioning display for merchandise in a drugstore. Dr. Scholl's goods might have graced this piece of funky furniture before it held Margaret's shoes. Now spray-painted black to offset her prized jeweled and feathered clompers, this tall holed and pegged plastic conversation piece goes flying, tossing off all the heavy platform shoes that graced it.

This is enough, thinks angry Margaret, as she watches the shoe rack tumble down. I cannot abide these junkies smashing the furniture. She leaps onto her platform shoes and rushes at him, suddenly wanting to smash his beautiful face in. Barely controlling her anger, Margaret grabs the purple bodice of her own dress and pushes the wimp Jimmy toward the door.

I can't believe she is taking this so seriously, thinks a surprised Jimmy. This is too silly. As Margaret pushes him backward, he smiles. Are we supposed to "have it out"? Settle this like men? This is *too* corny.

Margaret was relieved that she didn't have to hit him. Only as she threw his clothes out after him did she realize what happened and how frightened she was. What if he had fought back? He could probably knock my teeth down my throat if he wanted to, she thinks, as she flips up the rack and starts putting the shoes back on their pegs. She was so tired. Each shoe seemed to weigh ten pounds. The trouble with having possessions is that you have to handle things, place them, think about them, take care of them, she thinks slowly. I don't want to live in a mess here. That seemed more frightening to her than shooting up. It was the next step closer to being like the ones who came to her home to buy from Adrian; that the apartment, her home, should start to *look* like a shooting gallery.

Jimmy lost his hilarity as soon as the door slammed shut, and he found he was alone in the eerie hall on the twentieth floor. Locked doors and silence seemed all too familiar to him. He longed for screaming or accusations, anything instead. He was so alone. Not expecting any response, he called in to Margaret with an uncharacteristically timid voice.

Margaret thought Jimmy had gone when she heard him whine, "Are you going back to the Club?" He sounded like a little boy. Margaret was touched in spite of feeling drained. So many people feeding off her, sucking off her; she supposed that was part of the burden of being born a woman. After all, women have breasts: for feeding, for nurturing. So she answered, "I don't know." She was about to acquiesce, to care about him, when Jimmy asked about a cab.

When Margaret had answered him in a tone similar to his own, Jimmy's thoughts had raced ahead. His fear left him. He felt confident he would soon be safe at the Club. Expecting to share her cab (Margaret often took cabs because of her high shoes), Jimmy asked, "Are you going to take a cab?"

Margaret thought, I may be slow, but I'm not that slow. He just wants a ride to the Club, the slimy bloodsucker.

Her curt "Fuck you" made his fear come back.

Fashion Show

The shows always took forever. Each model had to have an intricate makeup designed for their face. The early birds would put all their makeup on, taking pains that it be model-perfect, only to have to wash it all off when the makeup artist arrived. Then, everyone would wait until the clothes arrived, and when they finally did, the designer would start switching their outfits around to go with the shoes. Because the shoes hardly ever fit.

On a rare occasion the models would get paid a token fee. But most did it for the status, and the free drinks, and the hope that the doorman wouldn't make them stand in line the next time they came to the Club. Because getting in the door of the Club had nothing to do with beauty. As a matter of fact, the opposite was true. "Fresh and wholesome" were not considered attributes by the keepers of this door. Often a taboo, tattoo, or exotic look could pass the portal, while pretty could not. Oddly enough, professional beauties were drawn to the Club. They had to be creative to be accepted, which meant respect for more than their dimples. So they worked for no fee in exchange for belonging.

The organizers, designers, and Club managers would all be shouting to hurry this, or hurry that; but the models more experienced in Club life knew there was plenty of time, because Margaret and Jimmy weren't even there yet. Margaret and Jimmy were late. The Club owner said that he wouldn't let Margaret and Jimmy go on, and the designer argued with him. This was all done very theatrically of course, but only the newer models—the straight ones— ever let on that they believed it. Everyone else knew the tired twins would go on at the last minute. It was all part of the show.

They arrived when Adrian was just finishing her song. Margaret had heard Adrian perform before, but she still felt guilty about missing her act. As the familiar lyrics reached Margaret's ears, she mouthed the words with her lover. "Just me and my rhythm box, me and my rhythm box, me and my rhythm boooaahhhhaahhhhx." Margaret felt emptied by the song. Perhaps it was some kind of self-preservation, that Margaret didn't hear the whole of Adrian's song. Where am I in that? she caught herself wondering. Then she berated herself for being so subjective. She was sitting in the "hair chair" being fixed up for the show. People were scurrying around her, pulling her hair, holding up clothes in front of her to get the "look" coherent. But under her chair Margaret was tapping her feet together. It's only art, it's only art, she repeated to herself over and over, clicking her heels together, and thinking of the Wizard of Oz.

She was so tired. The night was young; she still had to model, and all she wanted was to go to sleep. Was this ever fun? she wondered. Because Margaret was drained, it was unusually comforting to let the makeup artist do her face. Usually she would argue and get involved in any artistic endeavor that involved her face. But this artist was protective of her. When the photographer's rep had come over to confirm the shoot for the next night, the makeup artist said, "You are not supposed to be in here. Please leave." So tonight, it seemed comforting to let him do it for her. She had enough to think about.

Because Margaret was frightened. She had done a lot of shows. She knew there was a feeling that went along with modeling in the Club, the show, her whole lifestyle. But she was too tired, she couldn't remember what it was. She looked over at Jimmy. He always looked so confident. Maybe she could figure out what she was supposed to be feeling if she talked to him.

The photographer's rep had rambled on about shooting on Margaret's roof and the Empire State Building and what a good location her apartment was for the shoot. Then he had started in on Jimmy. The rep left finally, convinced that Jimmy was confirmed for the shoot the next evening. But Margaret knew him better than that. It was a good excuse to talk to him. He would probably think she was asking if he was coming over because of the fight they had had. "Are you coming over to my roof tomorrow night?" Margaret probed timidly. Jimmy looked at her, too cool to care, and snarled, "I'll decide that tomorrow night." Of course he's right, thought Margaret. I should have known. Who can tell what will happen from one day to the next?

Jimmy stood on the top stair of the platform on the stage and leaned against the wall. He looked out at the audience, down on the gyrating models, and lit a cigarette. The less you give them, the more they like it, he repeated to himself. Jimmy tried to ignore the hundreds of staring eyes, and took a deliberately casual step down the stair. As he exhaled, he remembered his first show. The fear had made him numb. He hadn't known what to do, so he did nothing. Afterward, everyone had commented on his minimalistic style. How he hated them for that. And they seemed to even like that he hated them. Modeling is so stupid, Jimmy thought as he inhaled the smoke from his cigarette. The more I don't model, the more they like it. People really like it when you treat them bad. The only thing that made him nervous when he modeled nowadays was when the cigarette would burn out before the outfit was finished. He was concerned that this was about to happen. The problem was that he just didn't know what to do with his hands. He couldn't keep them in his pockets because it would spoil the line of his jacket. Why can't I just show the outfit and get off the stage? Jimmy thought, frustrated. He looked over at Margaret doing her dance. How embarrassing, he thought disparagingly. Besides looking stupid, that dance she does takes too long. What do they see in it? How can they watch that spectacle? It seemed to go on forever, her twisting, turning, and jumping in those high shoes.

This is taking so long, Jimmy agonized. It's taking so long because of Margaret. Why do they ask her to model? I know why, he thought angrily. They're waiting for her to break her neck. Suddenly Jimmy realized the audience could be watching him watch Margaret. He was frozen. How awful! he thought. They might think that I like her, that I have a crush on her, and everyone knows she's queer. He longed to leave the stage. But he walked around it casually. His face revealing none of his turmoil. He didn't want to give anyone the impression that he was uncomfortable.

People had first asked Margaret to model because they

saw her dancing at the Club. She had just started moving one day, and a series of jerks, jabs, and jumps seemed to pour out of her body. She would feel it welling up in her and would take to the dance floor to get it out. Pretty soon people were asking her to "do her dance" and "dance in the show." That's when she had to start faking it. Because sometimes the feeling just wouldn't come. She knew that it didn't matter how she moved, as long as it wasn't anything that "went along" with how people did it normally. So she would do the kind of movements she always did, praying that it would happen, that she would "get it out." But now she was in front of all the people, and it seemed very quiet to her, even though the music was playing, she could hear mostly the clomping of her own feet. So she was working out that search in front of them, jerking and twisting and trying to find what was missing. Here she was, in front of her whole world, teetering on her shoes. At the end of the show she felt humiliated for letting them see her desperation and for trying to please them. And it was only at the end of the show that she could remember what was missing. It was her anger. And now she had a lot of it.

Adrian always went in the bathroom between events, in case someone wanted to score. She was really surprised that Margaret was hanging out with her, 'cause Margaret knew that's where she sold it, and Margaret wasn't that fond of the drug-selling bit. When Adrian had told her that she made her living from performing, it hadn't occurred to Adrian that Margaret would actually believe it. Looking at her babe now, hanging on her with that devoted expression, she could almost believe that Margaret could be so naïve. But there was really something slutty about her, something that made you question her admiring gaze. Still, it was flattering to have Margaret on her arm, especially right after the fashion show, when she could be soaking up the praise.

Margaret was truly sorry for missing Adrian's song. Adrian would never say it, but Margaret had felt she wanted her to watch. Margaret felt guilty and wanted to make it up to her. So she hung on Adrian in the traditional way, the way men like. It really made Margaret sick to her stomach, but she didn't know how else to make it up to her. It had always made the men happy.

Jimmy went into the bathroom to take a leak, and to see if Adrian would be in there selling. It came as a shock when he saw Margaret hanging on Adrian. Usually everyone was too cool for contact. They were so . . . intimate. As he went to the commode, he wondered what it would be like to have someone. Someone that it would be all right to be seen with, as a friend, someone to talk to. As he unzipped his fly, he felt very alone, even though they were a few feet away. For a moment, Jimmy was jealous. Then, as he released his urine, he remembered, Margaret isn't really someone you can be seen with. So much of what she does is . . . questionable.

As soon as she saw Jimmy enter the bathroom, Margaret knew she was gonna tell on him. Adrian was into punishing even when she didn't have a reason. So, of course, Adrian would join in; she wouldn't give him what he wanted. Margaret waited till just the right moment. Jimmy zipped up his fly, sauntered over, and asked for his fix. That's when she said, "He smashed up our place looking for it."

Jimmy was mad. He called her names. But Margaret didn't let them faze her. She felt vindicated. It's a bitch when a junkie has their supplier mad at them. Margaret felt elated. Everything was great until Adrian offered Jimmy's fix to her, to Margaret! Margaret could not believe it!

That's what she got for being nice to Adrian—to be treated like one of her customers.

Adrian knew it was a mistake as soon as she said it. She had only meant to make Jimmy squirm. To make him sweat over his portion of potion. But Margaret took her wrong. Adrian knew what was coming next. Margaret would find some scab with blow to punish her. Margaret knew that Adrian hated when she got drugs from other people. She was a dealer, she could get anything in trade; how did it look to have her girlfriend scrounging drugs from the scabs? Sarcastically Adrian said, "There's some guy on the dance floor offering coke to all the 'chicks,' why don't you ask him?" In a flash she knew she had made another mistake. You can't humiliate Margaret. The girl has no shame.

Her long public search paid off. The anger was exhilarating, came out in an even flow. It was better than a drug when Margaret got mean. The corny ones were the best to take it out on. They were even too scummy to be scabs. They were simple to spot.

Margaret stood on the lip of the dance floor. Adrian was right. This one you could spot a mile away. He was wearing jeans! Margaret wondered how he even got in the door. Probably in exchange for blow, she said to herself.

As usual, it was easy. Margaret danced a little in front of him, and then walked away and leaned on the wall. He came over and offered a toot immediately. Then came a hitch. He didn't want to do the blow in the Club. Now Margaret would have just walked away, except she wanted to hurt him worse than that. This was her world; he didn't belong here and should not pass through unscathed. But she could see his point. Margaret would never get busted in the Club. But someone like him, well, there were narcs all over that needed to make their quotas. He would be just the type they would take. Narcs wanted to be a part of nightlife as much as anyone, so they only ever busted scabs or corny ones who wandered in there. If they took him, he might mention Margaret to them too. So Margaret decided to break routine and take him to their place. That would really get to Adrian.

As soon as they left the Club, he started to talk. Idiot, Margaret thought to herself and then set him straight. "Do me a favor," she said sternly. "Don't try to make conversation, okay?" They walked in silence toward her place. When they got there, the scab attempted to ask some questions about the building's being deserted, but Margaret shut him up with a look that said it all. And he surprised her by not pushing it.

Once they got inside the apartment, he made the usual observations about the view while Margaret gathered her mirror and razor. It's nice to snort in comfort for a change instead of in alleys and smelly bathrooms, Margaret thought. She sat on the bed, put her mirror on her lap, and said, "Let's do it." She was only mildly impatient with him when he offered Quaaludes instead of laying cocaine out on the mirror. After all, they were 714s, which were impossible to find nowadays. Her "No, thank you" of course surprised him. Because these were vintage drugs. He said, "Have you ever had Quaaludes before?"

"I've taken more Quaaludes than you have aspirin. They don't excite me." Jesus, is this guy slow, thought Margaret. Do I look like someone who's never had a 'lude? I guess I should make it real clear to him. "If I want downs I can shoot heroin anytime I want. But I don't want smack, and I don't want Quaaludes. Where's the cocaine?" Margaret could not believe it when he said, "I have to call a guy."

She was falling asleep as it was. If she didn't get something "up," the evening would be over. "He'll be right over," said the boy. Oh, thought Margaret, taken aback.

This guy must be a dealer or a supplier or something, if he has runners. Adrian let addicts run drugs for her all the time, in exchange for their fix. If the guy has runners, he must have quality blow. The guy dialed, but the line was busy. Margaret got exasperated.

"That's just great. How long is this going to take?" she demanded. "Not long. What's your rush?" he replied, and proceeded to rub her leg. Margaret could not even react to such a lame attempt to come on to her. She just looked at his hand on her leg. "I'm going back to the Club to dance. Why don't you try your friend once more?" She hadn't even been civil to the creep and he imagined that she would touch his clammy flesh. Instead of dialing, the creep held the pills under her nose. Margaret said, "What are you gonna do, shove them down my throat? Why don't you call your friend?"

"You're a model, right?" he said. "Right," replied Margaret. She was thinking of the walk back to the Club if she dumped this troublesome outsider. After sucking on the flask all night, she had been counting on the coke to give her a lift into sobriety. Margaret really didn't know if she had the energy to make it back without a toot. "Yeah, I saw you in a show," said the boy. Margaret bit her tongue and said only, "Call." He ignored Margaret's comment. "You want to be an actress?" he said. "I *am* an actress," said Margaret. I'm acting like you are worthy of a reply, thought Margaret, trying to amuse herself. "I work on the soaps. My father works at MGM. He gets me work. I have a house in L.A. and a three-bedroom apartment here. It's a nice place. You want to go there?"

That, thought Margaret, is not even worthy of a response. She tried to remain calm. "No," she said. "I want you to call your friend." His reply made Margaret furious. He said, "My father can help you."

She wanted to strike him. Instead, all of her pent-up anger released in a steady stream from out her mouth. "What are you saying? Your father is going to help me break into show business? That's the corniest line I've ever heard."

"You don't want me to help you?" the guy reacted, disbelieving.

"You help *me?*" Margaret said incredulously. She hated him, everything he was, everything he stood for. That easy white male way of expecting achievement to fall in his lap. So privileged in the world, and for what? For being born with a penis. A fleshy stick which equaled instant respect whether deserved or not. "You're only a big deal 'cause your daddy is successful. Without him, you're nothing. You're just his baby boy."

Margaret enjoyed his surprise. I'll bet no one has ever talked to him that way, she thought triumphantly. He's been coddled all his life. His mother would probably have sucked his cock if she could.

"You're stupid," he said. "My father can get you a job acting. You're pretty enough. He'll do it if I tell him to. You should be nice to me. He'll do it for me."

Of course he will, thought Margaret, outraged. You were born to purchase women's souls with your daddy's charge card. How many out-of-work California actresses have sold their body for a glimmer of hope? He's never going to use this line again, she decided maliciously. "You just want to get laid. You'll say anything to get laid. You're just like everyone else from California. What do you have? A cock for a brain, baby?"

The anger was cleansing her. Suddenly her thoughts were clear, crystal clear, like taking crystal. "Who do you think you're dealing with? You think the Club is your playground? You think you can walk in and pick out a piece of candy? Nobody there is stupid enough to fall for your shit. There's no assholes there, 'cause we don't depend on our daddies and mommies for comfort." She imagined the verbal abuse was scarring his brain. She wanted to hurt him for all time, so he would never forget.

"Shut up!" he demanded.

"I'm a downtown girl, 'honey,' " Margaret said, reveling in her superiority.

"I can help you to be an uptown girl," he retorted.

She couldn't believe it. He still didn't get it! *"You* help *me?* Don't fuck with me, you asshole. You're just a baby. Why don't you fuck your father if he loves you so much?"

It happened so fast it didn't really register. She felt his fingers burrow into the flesh of her cheek and the dry, chalky objects in the back of her throat, blocking her breath. He slapped her face and said something to her, but she didn't really feel it, and she didn't really hear what he said. It was hard to believe that it happened at all except that she needed a drink to get the residue from the pills out of her throat. Then he was watching her. Margaret took a swig from her flask in a slow, purposeful manner, and tried to collect her thoughts. The verbal retaliation escaped her lips as soon as the Stoli had burned its way down her throat.

"Such a big man. What is that supposed to do? Make me fall apart and spread my legs? You need more than two Quaaludes to do that, baby. Why don't you go home to your momma?"

The blows fell in a steady rhythm across her cheeks and mouth. The pain was cumulative, like the effect when Novocain is wearing off. It was an unceasing, jarring attack. Slowly, it occurred to Margaret to fight back. She rose and pushed her long body into his compact chest, trying to flip him off the bed. His strength was a shock to her. He flipped her easy, despite the contrast in their sizes, and the next volley of blows made her ears ring. It had never occurred to Margaret that anyone would use violence against her. Gradually, she realized she was in trouble. Finally, it occurred to her to be afraid. And then it stopped.

Margaret had never wished for the presence of Adrian so heartily. Adrian would know what to do. "Adrian will be home soon," Margaret said, hoping he would believe it, wishing it were true herself. He replied, "It's only two o'clock." He was looking at her in a queer manner, as though beating her up were some form of love play. Margaret decided to play along to buy time. Smiling in a sweet, suggestive manner, she said, "Give me my flask . . . please." He murmured in surprise, "You want a drink?" and rubbed her leg in anticipation. Margaret pasted the smile on her face and let her breath carry a promise. "Yeah . . ." she said softly, ". . . yeah." When he turned to get the flask she planned her escape: throw the Stoli in his eyes, dive under the coat rack, and run to the elevator on the next floor before he could recover. Swallowing the burning liquid as he watched, Margaret knew she had to act fast. Throwing the clear alcohol in his eyes, she spit, "I want my vision to be blurred so I don't have to look at your face!" But that last insult cost her precious seconds and belied her own belief in her ability to escape.

The plan was a good one, but for the pills working so quickly. She dived out under the clothes rack and headed down the steep stairs, frightened that she would stumble in her high shoes. There was only one elevator; it had to be where she left it because they were the only people in the building. All she had to do was to catch it before he could get to her. But, nothing for supper but the contents of her flask sped the effect of the pills. Her feet were like lead weights; her legs moved in slow motion. Her mind was aware but she couldn't will her body to respond quickly. He grabbed her as she rounded the corner on the stairs. Margaret barely felt him slam her against the wall. The marble wall felt cool on her face as she slipped down. She remembered him ripping the crotch out of her pantyhose. It didn't hurt. Not that she could remember.

Paul Is a Junkie

When Margaret woke, she did not open her eyes. Her face felt petrified. She breathed deeply and lay still. The air smelled very clean in the well-ventilated hallway. There was a damp morning chill even though it was August. But she felt it only in her nose, with her breath. It must be cold, she thought. It was just beginning to get light out. She picked her face up off the cold stone step. She didn't think about how she had gotten there. Margaret concentrated on the details of each moment. First, she had to get her legs to work. She was lying head down with her legs upon the lip of several stair. Shifting her weight, she pulled her legs off the steps where stone had been kissing flesh, and willed the blood to go into the indentations in the skin of her thighs. She felt very loose-limbed, but not tired. Oddly enough, she felt like she could go forever without sleep. Usually after downs, she needed to slumber for at least a day. As Margaret pulled her legs close to her, she thought, Are these my legs? They didn't seem like they were attached somehow. She pressed her heels into her buttocks, and rolled her weight onto her shoes. She leaned her right shoulder into the grillwork of the stairs. Holding tight to the thin metal bars, she pulled herself up and hung her body over the banister. Hanging on the railing, she took a step up the stairs. She couldn't feel her legs, but they did work when she told them to. She could feel the lacquered wood of the banister slide under her fingers as the other leg joined her on the step. She pressed her lips on the wood to steady her swaying, and then took another step. It was like learning to walk again. She repeated the act, and noted each sensory perception until she reached the door of the apartment.

Relying more on her arms than legs, Margaret transferred her weight from the railing to the metal handles of the open door. She rode the door and it smashed into the wall. Lying against the plasterboard wall, she rolled until she reached the bathroom. Then she stretched to grasp the towel rack and pulled her body up the step into the bright light. Letting go of the towel bar, she stood for the first time that morning, and looked out the bathroom window over the tops of buildings.

The buildings were so close and bright, but hazy and empty. Most of her life she would wake up and see trees. The view didn't seem real to her. Margaret absentmindedly made her way forward while staring out over her hazy, greenless jungle. Her toe bumped the porcelain of the tub, and she let herself stumble into it. Drawing the plastic curtain she blocked out the unreal view. Margaret stretched for each faucet separately, turning both to the fullest possible turn. She closed her eyes to the wet. And the water washed her away.

The next time she opened her eyes, she thought her blood had turned blue and was running into the drain. But it was the dye from her hair and dress. Her shoes had swollen, the cork soles of her high wedgies were now too heavy to move. As she slipped them off, she remembered her pantyhose being torn. Rapidly she ripped off the leggings. Her dress was harder to remove; the turquoise satin stuck to her skin. It seemed forever before she could wiggle out of it. It was a relief to take off the tight black bra and the orange plastic necklace, which had been digging into her skin. Finally unclothed, Margaret noticed the blue stains on her skin. At first she thought they were bruises. She attacked the colored skin with a bar of soap. Then there were only blue suds for a long time.

Margaret was sitting in front of her makeup mirror smoking hash from the bird-claw pipe when she heard voices. It was Adrian and the man Paul, coming up the stairs. Margaret thought a lot about Adrian's customers, all of them. What their lives were like. Who they lived with. How they got to be users. Paul is a filmmaker, thought Margaret, that's why Adrian likes him so much. Adrian had a kind of comradery with Paul that she didn't allow with most of her customers. But that didn't mean he wasn't as hooked. He came regularly, had to have it. But Adrian wasn't as cruel to him as to the others; she gave it to him whenever he asked. He had to pay for it, of course, but he was the only one outside their peer group that she was nice to. Margaret always tried to figure out the reasons for the way people behaved. She thought maybe Adrian figured Paul would put her in one of his movies.

His girlfriend's name was Katherine. Adrian saw her once and said she was real straight, tall and graceful and straight. Adrian likes straight people, thought Margaret. It's some kind of perverse admiration. That's why she likes Paul, because his girlfriend is so straight and tall, and Adrian's so weird and small. For a while while they lived separately, Paul and Katherine. Then, Katherine had invited Paul to live with her, thought Margaret. Less rent, she said. Paul didn't want to at first. But then he gave in. It made sense, less rent. He left his large, cold loft. But the people who used to drop by his loft didn't feel comfortable going to Katherine's warm house. Many of the ideas Paul had for his films came from the conversations he had with those characters. He was fascinated by them, and they loved him. He treated them like they were anybody else. They would just drop by. Katherine hated that. No one realized that was an important part of Paul's life. After all, most of them were lowlifes and derelicts.

The other thing was Paul's equipment. He didn't know where to put his editing machine in Katherine's apartment. It didn't seem to go in there. When Paul started to hock it, Katherine asked him about it. Paul said it was outdated, which it was. Secretly she wasn't sorry when the machines started to disappear from the apartment. They had looked so strange next to her couch. Paul always told her, and believed it himself, that his next movie he would rent better equipment.

Everyone likes Katherine, thought Margaret. She is like the perfect person: understanding, talented, and good-looking. Everyone thought she would be good for Paul, who had an impulsive streak. Paul was fascinated by people, all kinds of people, the kind of people most call losers. He had gotten acclaim for his movies, but they never made any real money. Sixteen-millimeter films about the cruelty of the capitalistic system usually don't. But the art crowd loved them. No one seemed to notice that Paul never paid for drinks at bars, or reciprocated when people took him to dinner. Paul was a great conversationalist. He created rare moments. He even made shooting up heroin sound reasonable and attractive, thought Katherine.

Paul was giving her a demonstration on how to shoot up. Katherine had had a good day. The illustrations she had completed for the book on antique toys had all been accepted. She was determined to have a pleasant evening, celebrate, and not let Paul upset her. All the paraphernalia of drug abuse was spread out on her kitchen counter. Paul has a really sick sense of humor, she thought. He used to love to shock her. Katherine hoped that was what he was up to now. He said, "First you heat it." Katherine opened the refrigerator and helped herself to a glass of white wine.

The heroin looks clear when heated, like the sugar glaze you put on a cake, thought Katherine. This is interesting, but I shouldn't give him the impression that I approve. He's been behaving strange lately. "It's dangerous, Paul. I don't want you to do it anymore," Katherine warned pleasantly.

Paul was really excited. He wanted her to have a good time. Especially since he wasn't holding up his end financially. It was the experience of a lifetime and he wanted to be the one to give it to her. "Don't be afraid. You only say that because you haven't experienced it. It's like nothing else. What have you got to lose?" he coaxed excitedly. Paul was obsessed with being her first, the first one to make her high. No one ever forgets their first high, he thought happily. You can forget a lover, but not an encounter with this beast.

She wanted to say, "We still have a chance. Give it up, Paul. Pull yourself together." But he had heard it all before, and had stormed out the door, returning a full day later sick and irritable. Katherine was determined to have a good time. Every evening had been painful, had ended in argument, and broken things. Tonight, she wanted it to be like it used to be. Tonight she wanted them to be special to each other. She said calmly. "It's self-destructive."

"That's media propaganda," Paul retorted. "People have been using opiates for centuries. In ancient Egypt, Greece, Rome, India, China, everyone used opiates, and nobody thought it was destructive or dangerous. They didn't think it was immoral to be euphoric."

"And all those civilizations are destroyed now," said Katherine in a soothing manner. Such a bright man, she thought. Such a kind, clever, intelligent man. Does he really believe what he is saying? Maybe I'm wrong. Maybe he's not an addict, she tried to tell herself. Can it be that he's not hooked? Often he leaves me in the middle of the night to go and get his drugs. Can it be that simple? That he enjoys being "euphoric"?

"What are you talking about?" said Paul, smiling. "In this country at the turn of the century in every drugstore you could buy a heroin derivative to cure your ills." She sounds like a naïve housewife, thought Paul. She doesn't realize how many of her friends are users; all of them artists, all "up and coming." "And all the housewives used it for everything. They loved it," he went on enthusiastically. She is the motherly type, he thought. She would have lovingly used a drug to ease the pain of a loved one. He could imagine her standing over his bed wearing a white dressing gown. As she leans into him, her head blocks the available light and her hair glows on the fringes like a halo. She administers the "medicine" to him; the smell of her warm body and the drug intermingle. No one would have thought she was evil, he told himself, they would think she was an angel. An angel stopping the pain. "Everybody wants euphoria; what's wrong with that?"

A housewife—that's what he is calling me, that's what he thinks of me, thought Katherine, enraged. That I'm square, bourgeois. That I'm an artisan, but not an artist. Too straight, not willing to suffer for it. If that's what I am, then I accept it, she thought angrily. I am successful enough to support this household, and this man. I get money for my art work, but that doesn't mean I have to take these insults. "I am not a housewife at the turn of the century and I don't want heroin in my house," she said firmly.

"It's not just for pleasure. I use it to open my blocked thought passages. Cocteau wrote great fantasy literature while high on opium," said Paul.

How can such a bright man delude himself so? thought a shocked Katherine. He hasn't done anything, not even an interview, since he started taking this drug. He's not going to make films, or write any poems while he's high. He's just going to pass out! How can he compare himself with Cocteau? "Cocteau was Cocteau before he ever did drugs," she said sadly. Katherine watched as Paul looked at her, surprised. He really doesn't get it, thought Katherine. Poor Paul, my poor Paul. He really believes he's like Cocteau.

"What's that supposed to mean?" said Paul. Is she calling me a loser? he thought, panicked.

"That it won't help you," said Katherine. For the first time Katherine thought about a dry-out clinic. I hadn't realized it was so serious, she thought. He has really lost touch with reality. Paul doesn't even have insurance, she thought, concerned and wondered how she was going to pay for a clinic. Then she became angry. How artistic! she thought sarcastically. No health insurance. Suddenly she noticed him pulling the clear liquid into the needle with the syringe. She hadn't really believed he would do it. She was stunned by the horror of it. Did he really expect her to watch him shoot heroin in her kitchen?

"Bitch," mumbled Paul. "You always have to throw your success in my face." I was blind enough to think she would shoot up with me, he thought, disappointed. It's a good thing I'm going to be high in a moment or I would be really depressed. I thought it would be romantic, shooting together. I was even going to share my needle with her. I never share my needle with anyone. But she can't even appreciate that.

Paul wrapped the belt around his arm and slipped the end through the metal buckle. He pulled his belt tight and put it in his teeth. His veins came up fast. His body was ready for it. His hand shook with excitement. Through clenched teeth he said, "Help me. Hold this for me." He wanted her to hold the belt tight so he could steady his quivering shooting hand. I have good veins but my hand always shakes when I get this excited, noticed Paul.

Suddenly Katherine knocks the needle out of Paul's shaking hand. A shocked Paul compulsively observes its path across the shiny floor. It didn't break! he thinks gleefully as it stops bouncing. A shadow appears over the fragile object, then a high-heeled foot crunches the delicate glass on the kitchen tile. She's stepping on it! he realizes. Astonished, Paul seizes her torso, squeezing her limbs, and demands, "What are you doing?!"

"I'm sorry, Paul. I did it because I love you," Katherine says earnestly. For a moment she thought he was going to break her arm. The pressure of his muscular fingers on her slender limbs was becoming unbearable. Then Paul unexpectedly let go.

Paul hadn't listened to what Katherine had said. He was already thinking about the trip to the Club to get more dope. And then he found Adrian and now he's here! It seemed like she had gone to sleep, and they had arrived and entered her dream. Only it's my dream, thought Margaret, gratified, I made it. And I'm not asleep, she insisted cheerfully. I feel as though I will never have to sleep again. Margaret tried to feel at ease, and she would have, if not for the presence of the man. Having that Paul here, in this room, feels very strange, thought the dazed blonde.

Then Adrian said, "Turn around, go over by her, and stay put." It frightened Margaret that Adrian sent the man over to her. Margaret had felt that Adrian would protect her from . . . from her own clients? Margaret admonished herself, She always sends the clients over here while she takes the powder out of its hiding place. It was Margaret's unofficial job to distract them, to talk to the customers so they wouldn't dare think about peeking. But this one stood very close. He was staring at her strange. Paul said, "Who are you?"

Immediately Adrian asserted, "Leave her alone." There! I'm not imagining it, thought Margaret. He is weird about me. Adrian feels it too. Does he think I'm a junkie too? That I'm like him and have come here to score? "I live here," said Margaret, wanting to dispel any idea he might have about common interests. And she pulled the damp towel off her wet head to cover her exposed shoulders.

But the man kept staring at her "like that." "Are you her girlfriend?" Paul insisted.

"What difference does it make?" answered Margaret, as nastily as she could. Why is he so interested in my connection to Adrian? thought a panicked Margaret. Why is he looking at me "like that"? Maybe he's just sad about his own girlfriend, Katherine, Margaret soothed herself.

"I'm just curious. Do you like girls better than men?" said the smiling man.

Is he calling me names? What right does he have to question my behavior? thought Margaret condescendingly. He's not one of us. "I'm always curious about people who have to make those kind of sexual definitions," she answered.

"What do you mean?" asked the man.

"Homosexual, heterosexual, bisexual . . . it really depends on the person. Whether or not I like someone doesn't depend on what kind of genitals they have, as long as I find them attractive. Don't you think?" Isn't he an artist? thought Margaret. Isn't he supposed to know this?

"No. I don't want to fuck a man," he said.

He was moving closer! Margaret delicately leaned away from him. "I don't . . ." he whispered seductively. She froze. Don't move, she told herself. He shouldn't know that it matters. He's only trying to get a reaction, she rationalized frantically. "Okay, that's your business," she murmured as nonchalantly as possible.

"So you like both men and women then, huh?" he replied.

Margaret could feel his breath on her neck. He was so close. Don't get nervous, he's just a junkie, she assured herself. When she had complained to her girlfriend about customers coming in and out at all hours when she wasn't dressed, Adrian had told her that junkies were harmless. That they couldn't have an erection. This was something she thought of regularly; whenever the visitors came during sleeping hours. It comforted her now. "What difference does it make to you?" she said, smiling to herself. "You're a junkie. You can't get it up anyway."

"How do you know?" he said ominously.

Margaret felt very vulnerable, even though Adrian was in the room. "Leave me alone," she said. She wanted to scream it. What am I talking to this creep for? she asked herself. He'll construe it as interest. It seemed forever until Adrian came over with the little plastic bag.

Adrian said, "It's a good count," and handed it to him.

As Paul paid her, Margaret sighed with relief. Soon he will be gone, she thought. But he didn't leave. Margaret's protests didn't make any difference. He wanted to use Adrian's needle. Adrian was letting him stay. To let someone shoot in the apartment and use her needle was a big deal for Adrian. It was against Adrian's own policy. On the other hand, besides never brushing her hair in front of Margaret the only thing Adrian had never done in front of her was to shoot up. Margaret had seen Adrian high before, but she really didn't know if Adrian was shooting it. Maybe she doesn't really ever use her needle anyway, thought Margaret hopefully, maybe she only sniffs it. Even so, it was an unusual comradery being shown for this outsider.

"Your girlfriend is pretty, but she's a bitch," Paul said. "She's just an uptight Wasp cunt from Connecticut," Adrian replied jocularly. "You know, it takes her about two hours to get ready to go out." They spoke as if Margaret wasn't in the room. Maybe I'm not here, thought Margaret. I feel numb. But I should go through all the motions, just in case, so they don't see that there's something wrong with me. People can smell fear. Even though I was trying to cover it, the man came right over here and was smelling me. She scolded herself, I shouldn't have let them see.

Maybe we're all part of a large experiment. Someone could be watching us for a study. The thought was comforting. There was sense in existing after all. The junkie Paul was over by the window. She was trying to block it out. He had heated the junk and was cinching his arm with Margaret's bright green sash. Anyone could see him if they wanted to. He was right in front of the largest hypodermic of them all. If someone on top of the Empire State Building wanted to, they could see him through those machines. Twenty-five cents for a look at the man taking drugs. Paul was sweating and shaking. His hand isn't very steady. What if he misses his vein? thought Margaret, panicked. He could die in here. He needs a fix so bad he's not even going to wait until his hand is steady. Doesn't anyone notice it? Why don't they do something if they're watching? Scientists don't do anything but watch, thought Margaret, excited. Yeah, a scientist looking for aliens; a scientist looking for aliens looking for drugs. Paul inserted the needle and squeezed the warm liquid into his bulging vein. Margaret tried to block it out; she closed her eyes, searching for a daydream.

The stewardess stared at the person. She couldn't believe that she hadn't noticed it before. The largest man she had ever seen was crammed into his seat and having a terrible dream. The plane hit an air pocket and bumped along, but instead of waking him, it seemed to aggravate his condition. He was jerking, twitching, mumbling, and groaning. The person next to him looked quite upset. "Would you like a cocktail?" the stewardess asked the middle-aged lady in an attempt to placate her. "No, thank you. I don't drink; but if I did I would have one now. Only I don't believe I would be able to get my tray down," she replied. It was true. The man's legs were so long that his knees pinned her tray up. Well, the stewardess thought, I'd better wake him. She will have to get her tray down to eat her fake food. The stewardess leaned over the lady to get a closer look at the passenger. He had the largest head she had ever seen on a person. It creeped her out to rouse him. He had such a strange expression on his face it looked as though he could be wearing a Halloween mask.

Johann Hoffmann was surprised and annoyed that the stewardess woke him from deep sleep to ask him if he wanted a cocktail. He had had little rest since his decision to leave the scientific institute, and knew that by the time he checked into a hotel it would be past twelve. So much depended on his diligence and speed, and he knew what havoc the effects of alcohol could wreak, both from a professional and a personal standpoint. His father had been an alcoholic; his mother too had had her bout with drink. And he knew how prone he was to its liberating properties. That's what they had said at the laboratory when he had told them about the study of the alien, that Johann should go to the dry-out camp. So much was at stake here—not just his reputation as a scientist, but the lives of many people. He couldn't tell if the aliens would propagate as they found more victims or not. He would have to gather more data to determine that. But certainly they would strike again. He looked at the American woman before him, wearing the odd uniform, waiting for his reply. He wondered if she lived in New York City, and if she could be the next victim.

"Get ready to go. Don't sulk; you should be happy Paul came. He gave us some money to get some lunch. So start getting ready to go out." Adrian looked at Margaret as she spoke. She looked so nice without all that makeup on, like when she first met her. It was easy to forget the cooze disappeared with a scab early last night when you looked at that innocent face. Adrian was very relieved when she had come home and Margaret was alone. She had stalled Paul for a long time, 'cause she was scared to bring him home. Scared to find Margaret and some scab together; that would be really humiliating. Because Paul's girlfriend isn't like that. Adrian had told Margaret how clean Katherine was. That's what I thought I was getting when I hooked up with Margaret, thought Adrian, a real, classy girl. But there she is, sitting in a pink slip, in front of the whole world.

Margaret had forced herself to sit calmly, when Paul and Adrian had walked in the door. Her impulse had been to hide in a small, dark place, but that would have given her away. They would have known that there was something wrong with her. She felt safe in front of her own makeup mirror, in the big metal chair. It was her chair, her place. No one else sat in her chair in front of the mirrors. It seemed like a very big job to rise and change her clothes. I'm so big, she worried. I would be noticed. If I stand up they might look at me; he would watch. It's better not to do anything at the moment. She studied her reflection. It was a stranger staring back at her. Who is that person? Is that me? Margaret wondered. Adrian's suggestion that Margaret cross the room and get dressed, passed from her mind. Do I really have so many freckles? she thought, distracting herself. Then, a frightening notion passed through her mind before she could suppress it. What if he nods out before Adrian gets rid of him? Margaret panicked. That would be the worst. If Adrian let him stay. Her body froze. She desperately tried to think of something else.

The cab driver was surprised when the tall foreign man asked for the Hotel Breslin. He had never even heard of the damn place. Usually, you could catch a beeline fare to midtown from the airport and turn a profit without much hassle. He considered throwing the sucker out of his cab to try and get a tourist with more exclusive tastes going somewhere vaguely familiar. But the presence of the airport taxi license examiner dissuaded him. The foreigner didn't speak the entire journey into Manhattan. Whenever the cabbie would try to speak to the guy to pass the time, the tall stranger wouldn't answer. Then, a few moments later, the giant would shout through the hole in the see-through partition, "Three-ohh . . . three-ohh . . . *very* close to the Empire State Building." He's probably hard of hearing, the cab driver thought. When they arrived at the hotel, the lobby was deserted. This confirmed his suspicions about the nature of this hotel. He figured if he hadn't heard of it, it had to be weird; but this fare hadn't looked like the depraved type. The size of the tip the guy gave him came as a pleasant surprise. Not that it was huge or anything. But the guy hadn't wanted to put his case in the trunk. That was a sure sign of a poor tipper, someone who didn't want to pay the fifty-cent trunk charge. The man held onto his great, strange valise like he was gonna be mugged in the cab. A true paranoid tourist if he ever saw one, thought the driver as he watched the joker finally enter the hotel lobby. The driver sat in his cab and watched him lumber up the checkered corridor. "Probably thinks the Empire State Building is a distant relative," he said out loud. He caught himself laughing at his own bad joke, and shook his head. The night shift was getting to be too much for him.

Margaret sat staring in the mirror at Paul's reflection as he administered the drug. This makeup mirror belonged to my Great-Aunt Mary, Margaret thought to herself. She turned and looked to the Empire State Building. He's up there right now, the model reminded herself. The scientist took his great valise up to the observation deck, and he's there right now. He has a special instrument in his case that helps him look for junkies. Margaret's gaze dipped for a moment. Paul was still pressing the warmed liquid into his vein. So slow . . . so slowly. Aunt Mary's sister had been named Margaret. She died very young. Was that why Mary left this piece of furniture to me? thought Margaret. The machine has an earpiece that is beeping in a steady rhythm in his large ear. It's bright in the sun and beside him a newborn infant lies in it's mother's arms. But the scientist doesn't notice. He scans the cityscape, looking down at the office buildings, warehouses, and terraces, through his specially modified telescope. Beep . . . beep . . . beep . . . I wonder if he can see the women who sunbathe naked next door? thought Margaret. It wasn't actually next door: it was

blocks away. But it is the closest building facing our roof
and the windowed door. This scientist isn't looking for
naked girls, he is looking for aliens, thinks Margaret happily. An alien presence attracted to heroin. Suddenly the
beeps get faster; he slows his telescopic instrument and
concentrates on that area. Then he sees Paul. A hunched-
over junkie with my bright green sash binding his muscles.
Paul with a needle in his arm in the window of our roof.

Lunch with Adrian

Jimmy had told Margaret about his cat. He was at her place
and someone had told him on the telephone that his cat had
died, and he got very upset. He kept saying, "I should have
helped her bury it." He went to meet his mother once or
twice a week for lunch. That's when she would give him
money. Margaret knew that, because after his lunch Jimmy
would come directly to their place to buy the drug or pay
Adrian what he owed her. Sometimes Adrian let him owe
her, sometimes not. Adrian enjoyed being perversely erratic that way. Jimmy's mother, Sylvia, had an important job
that paid well, at least it seemed that way; because Jimmy
and his Mother always went somewhere really nice for
lunch. Whereas, Margaret and Adrian always went to some

truck stop, diner, or dive. I wonder where we're headed now, thought a sulky Margaret.

She was walking with Adrian down the bright street. Her shoes were lower than what she usually wore, but still, she didn't want to walk so far. Because she was sore. Her legs and ankles hurt her. I wonder what that is from? Probably from dancing in the show, she told herself.

When they finally got to the restaurant, it was another diner. Margaret tried not to be disappointed. Anyway, it's just as well we don't go somewhere too fancy, Margaret rationalized. You never know how Adrian will behave. As they sat down in the booth, Adrian looked directly at Margaret. Suddenly Margaret felt very vulnerable. She felt naked. Adrian had gotten upset when it took her so long to put her clothes on, so Margaret had left the apartment without any makeup. After the man left it only took me a few minutes to get ready, thought Margaret proudly. Anyway, it's just as well we didn't go somewhere nice, she told herself. I don't even have any makeup on.

As usual, his mother had picked a very elegant place to meet. His mother had excellent taste; she wanted it to seem effortless. Whenever Jimmy would compliment her on her clothes or possessions, she would shrug it off just as though wasn't important to her. "Where did you get that suit, Sylvia?" Jimmy would ask. His mother would look at him pointedly and reply, "I don't remember." There was always so much tension between them it seemed to Jimmy that he earned the money she gave him. Their lunches seemed like so much work.

Every time I see this boy he seems obsessed by my clothing, thought Sylvia. His own appearance is so studied and strange. Jimmy was wearing a bright blue jacket over a stylized shirt and tie that looked like it could be part of a costume. Sylvia appreciated that he dressed up to meet her for lunch, but he wore so many clothes for a young person. In the summer, most young people tend to wear less clothing, Sylvia had observed. Because they spend so much time outdoors, she thought, staring at him. But Jimmy is so pale. "Aren't you a little warm in those clothes?" she inquired of her son.

"No, Momma," Jimmy responded warily. She was always called Sylvia, particularly in public. She hated to be called Momma. By calling her that, Jimmy hoped to divert her attention from his appearance. Why should she care how I dress? he thought suspiciously. She never took an interest before. But the reason he wore so many clothes was because of the marks. One time he wore a T-shirt to lunch, and it made him nervous even though it had long sleeves. It made him feel more comfortable if there were as many layers as possible between his mother and the needle marks on his arms. Jimmy figured if he was going to sweat it was better to be from the heat. There wasn't much you could hide from this mother if she wanted to see it.

"I'm sorry I didn't help you. I've just been real depressed," he uttered quietly. Jimmy was truly sorry that he hadn't helped her. It must have been a terrible thing for her to do all by herself, he thought. "What are you depressed about?" asked Sylvia. Intensely he replied, "I should have helped you bury her, you know?"

"Concentrate on your career, whatever it is you're doing," Sylvia said. Have I really given birth to this weird person? she thought, dumbfounded. Doesn't he know that the vet takes care of the body of the animal? What can be going on in that mind of his? She had been relieved when Jimmy seemed to take an interest in modeling. It is healthy for a child to focus on a career instead of only scholastic goals, she reasoned. Granted, modeling is a relatively temporary career, she ruminated, but it's better than these

young people who go to school forever. The perpetual
student was a subject many of her peers discussed with her
over lunch. After all, they agreed, college is nothing like the
real business world. Jimmy's grades have dropped since
he's been interested in fashion, she thought, but according
to my friends, modeling is a very time-consuming profes-
sion. At first, apparently, they never make any money. But
then they make quite a bit, after the initial testing. Still, she
wondered, how can he make money in fashion, dressed the
way he is? I suppose that's the newest fashion trend. She
sighed.

"Remember the time she fell in the bucket of paint, and
we had to fish her out? And she couldn't breathe. Then I
had to put baby oil all over her fur . . ." Jimmy said emphatically. Could his mother have forgotten how they had
kneeled together on the porch and she had gently wiped
the tiny kitten's eyes and nose so it could see and breathe?
Had she really forgotten?

"It was only a cat. Why do you let it upset you so?" said
Sylvia, panicked. He seems so weak and young, she
thought. He is supposed to be a man already, and here he
is, whining about that cat. It was old; he couldn't have
expected it to last forever. English literature is probably not
a good major for someone so dreamy. He is dreamy,
thought Sylvia, and so very good-looking. He should do
well with the modeling.

"You must be real upset about it, Mom," he said sarcastically. Jimmy stared at his mother. She didn't even react to
his mockery. Even when he called her Momma she hadn't
gotten upset. It was as though he had not spoken at all.

"I have a free evening tonight. Maybe we should get
together," Sylvia suggested. "I've been meaning to talk to
you for a long time. Find out what you're doing, what
you've been up to. Come over for dinner?" Sylvia looked at

her son. She really knew nothing about him, it seemed. Maybe he isn't so strange, she thought hopefully. Maybe if we get together in my home for a change, it will be different.

Jimmy panicked. His mother wanted him to come over for dinner. She would ask him questions! In that intimate setting, can I really lie to her? he asked himself. When he was younger he had never been able to lie to his mother. She always found him out. With relief, he remembered the fashion shoot on Margaret's roof. "I have an appointment with a fashion photographer. I can't get out of it," he said to her with a blank face.

"I'm glad your career is going so well," remarked Sylvia. She tried to reason with herself. He has a prior appointment; don't feel rejected by it. But it didn't work. She felt terrible. What I need is a man, Sylvia consoled herself. Being a workaholic is good for business, but not so nice when you go home alone every evening. I'll try and flush out an old beau or something, she decided. Sylvia was determined not to be alone by nightfall.

Adrian snapped her fingers in front of Margaret's lifeless eyes. "Eat your food," she said. Margaret stared at the sandwich on her plastic plate. I should eat all the food on my plate, she remembered. You should leave just a little, but it's rude not to eat most of it. Margaret half wondered if there were exceptions to the rule. If it made any difference if you couldn't taste anything. But she didn't feel like breaking any rules today. She didn't want to take any more chances. So she chewed on the sandwich, even though she couldn't understand what flavor it was.

Adrian wondered what Margaret had been thinking about. She had been staring off into space for a long time. Margaret doesn't even notice I'm here! She's probably thinking about that guy she left with last night, Adrian fumed. What else would make her all moony-eyed like that? She probably does have a new lover. She sure doesn't seem too interested in me, Adrian thought angrily.

Margaret looked at her girlfriend. Suddenly the garbled words spilled out of Margaret's mouth. "Last night . . . that guy . . . he was . . . Where were you? Ohh! Why didn't you come home?" She gasped for breath. Her heart pounded furiously. "He made me . . . He put, pills. I couldn't . . ."

"Do I look like a priest?" interrupted Adrian. "I know you can't control yourself. So you had a good time. Don't pretend it's my fault 'cause I didn't come home. I knew you were there with that guy." Adrian spoke nonchalantly, as though she didn't care. There was no way she was gonna let the bitch know she was jealous. That would give her too much satisfaction.

Margaret was stunned. She was so busy trying to block out the barrage of unpleasant memories that she couldn't focus on what Adrian was saying. She was trying not to remember him hitting her. "He raped me," she whispered.

Adrian could not believe the nerve of the bitch. What a bad liar, she thought. Some women are just like that, loose like that. My mother is like that too. Margaret is just approachable. I should have known, she took to me so fast. What a story! How can she expect me to believe that that little guy could rape big Margaret? Adrian had seen the kid on the dance floor. She had secretly watched how easily Margaret had picked him up. He wasn't much bigger than me, she thought quietly. Just the right size for me. "So some guy fucked you. Big fucking deal. Eat your food. Apple pie . . . mmmmmmmmm," said Adrian.

Margaret was still. But she felt herself moving, shifting in space, although she was still sitting in her seat. Suddenly she was in her tree, sitting in the top boughs waving in the wind. It was her tree because she was the only one of the girls who could climb it, really climb it, not just hang from the accessible lower boughs. She had a place at the very top, near the hard green fruits, where the limbs were light but still strong enough to support her weight. Margaret would go there to eat her breakfast. In the summer, before she was even awake, she would methodically make herself a cinnamon toast and go to her place. Everyone was impressed with how high and how long she would sit there. They would stand at the bottom and talk about her with awe. But Margaret never told. She never told them that she was up there so long because she was frightened to come down. As she looked at Adrian, Margaret could feel the tree swaying under her. She wondered what she was doing sitting across from this strange person in this terrible place. She tried to explain why she didn't belong there. "My mother used to bake five or six apple pies at once and put them on the porch to cool. We had an apple tree in our backyard. We'd come in from playing and the porch would be filled with steam. But we couldn't have any pie until after dinner. But even after dinner—the pies were deep—they'd still be hot. I always burned my tongue. My mom would fix them with vanilla ice cream." Margaret could feel the cool cream soothing the acetic burning in her mouth.

This cunt knows I was sent to the home, and she has to brag about her family life? thought Adrian bitterly. She gets all the guys, all the luck, it's so easy for her. Well, what do you expect? She even looks like the spoiled type. At least she used to, before she fucked up her hair. "You were lucky, baby, she sounds like a real angel," the dealer replied.

Sylvia got nervous when she thought about her nights alone. Often her body felt as though it was betraying her with its need. As if she was a helpless teenager, she would be stricken; a relentless fever would wash over her. Sylvia wondered what curse had been put on her that she should be so utterly hungry and so utterly manless. She was a strong woman, that she knew. But sometimes the fear crept in. The fear that it was too late, she would never get a man. She had spent her youth competing in their world, and now she would pay. God was punishing her. She smiled. Punishing me with hormones; what a silly, old-fashioned idea, she said to herself. She pushed it away, but the fever remained. The hotter the fever, the more reasoning is required to convince myself that I'm not being punished, she reflected. Sylvia looked at the boy before her. His good looks soothed her now. He was, after all, her son. Pre-fever. Conceived in innocence, at that moment he looked as pure as his conception. She said fondly, "You know, last time you came by the studio . . . When was that?"

"Six months ago."

He seemed so cold. Sylvia felt unusually fragile. "Well, I . . . Remember there were a lot of people there? . . . Anyway, everyone asked if you were my brother."

What does that mean? thought Jimmy wildly. She wishes she wasn't my mother? She wants to be my sister. And everyone says that weird Margaret is like me too. They all expect me to be their brother. She must sense that I don't have strong thoughts like a man should. That's why she doesn't want to be my mother. She never did. She never acted like a mom should. Well, I don't want her either. I wish I was never born.

"Of course you are my sister, Momma."

Jimmy's sarcasm cut her like a knife. She wished that his meanness would show on his unflawed face. She could imagine the gnarled crevices that would form there, if God weren't dead. She matched his sarcasm. "You really are gorgeous, you know that?" Leaving seemed appropriate to her, but she paused, not wanting to mention it, because of the onslaught of guilt that might ensue. But when Jimmy, her creature, the monster from her loins, was about to speak, she mentioned the time, to cut off any other injurious phrases that might come from his perfectly formed mouth. "I have to run."

"Can I have some money?" Jimmy habitually asked for money whenever a woman mentioned his looks. It was automatic behavior. As soon as he had said it, Jimmy cringed inside. He hadn't wanted to say it at that moment. It was wrong, immoral. For a moment it felt as though he had done something irrevocable. So when she said she would send him a check, he was relieved. That would be his punishment. Because he really needed cash.

"I really need it, you know?" he croaked. I'm sorry, Momma, he thought to himself. I'm sorry for everything.

"Can I give you a lift uptown, Jimmy?" After I've transported him I've done my duty, thought Sylvia. I've given him money, fed him, what more can I do? Jimmy smiled strange at her. His charisma was undeniable.

"No, no," he responded, "I'm going down."

Adrian smiled roguishly. She held her fork like it was a jackknife. "I took care of everyone. It was me that was takin' care of everybody. I used to buy frozen apple pies at the store and heat them up for me and my little brother." Her smile disappeared—"I had to change his diapers"—and reappeared larger than life. "But my mom was great. Listen! Once when they let her out, it was cool. It was great! So she went out with this guy, this really straight guy. They went to a real expensive restaurant; best in town! Right? And he was wining and dining her. Then all of a sudden"— swiftly Adrian crouched in her seat like an animal readied to spring—"all of the sudden, man . . ." Dramatically Adrian slowly rose up on the seat of their booth. She felt alive, energized, like when she was on stage. "She stood right up on the balcony . . ." This will show that smug bitch, the singer thought to herself, relishing her own performance. "And she looked out over all the people and said, 'I'M JESUS CHRIST. I BAPTIZE YOU IN THE NAME OF THE FATHER, THE SON, AND THE HOLY GHOST.' And she pissed on everybody!"

For a moment Margaret expected a torrent of urine to erupt from Adrian's lifted skirts. But her keeper relaxed and sat down.

"Jesus," said Adrian, as she settled into her seat, "It must have gone in their fuckin' food and everything. Can you beat that?"

Margaret looked at Adrian blankly. She wondered if the story was true. Adrian was waiting for her reaction. At least we weren't in a nice place, where everyone would have noticed, thought Margaret gratefully. "Then what happened?" Margaret uttered obligingly. She knew when to humor her moody mate.

"Then they threw her back in. They split me and my brother up. Put us in the home. I used to break out and run home, and they would throw me back in," said Adrian matter-of-factly.

Margaret remembered the stories she had told her about the home. Adrian had been like the leader of a group of girls. Rival gangs, bars on windows, mock wedding ceremonies for girl-couples in the church when the nuns were out, scarring for marking the girls who belonged to her; she had her own gang. She was the leader, the head of the group. Why would she want to leave? thought Margaret. "Why?" At least she got respect.

Adrian smiled sweetly. "Well, my dad is a sweetie pie. I love him a lot. But he couldn't handle it." Adrian didn't want to tell about the other parts, to think about the scary parts, the parts when her mother would get out. She tried to imagine her small, smiling Italian daddy without a wine bottle in his hand. "He used to sing to me though. He could sing great."

They didn't give her much, but they gave her the desire to sing, thought Margaret. Adrian is an incredible performer. "I know you were great tonight," Margaret said sincerely.

Adrian stared at Margaret, her head exploding with anger. This bitch has so much nerve, she thought. This Wasp cunt was off fuckin' some guy, didn't even bother to show for my song, and now she's trying to smooze me. Impulsively Adrian takes a swipe at Margaret, flicking up her stiff bleached bangs. "Why'd you have to fuck up your hair? You look like shit."

"That's what Owen always says," Margaret retaliated. Any mention of Owen usually made Adrian back down. Suddenly Margaret remembered. She had an appointment with him! She had an appointment with Owen! She had only said it to hurt Adrian, but she really was supposed to meet him today. Margaret sucked in her breath in fright. Was she too late? "Huuhh. Owen," Margaret groaned guiltily.

"What?" demanded Adrian. What now?! she thought. What else can this slut be up to?

"I was supposed to meet Owen," Margaret admitted. Margaret didn't let Adrian see her relief. Owen was her friend. He would help her. She was feeling alone in the world. How many times had she been troubled? How many times had her mentor given her advice? Then she panicked at the thought that she might miss him, that she would be too late.

"Is he coming to our place?" Adrian asked, with a grimace. I knew she had something up her sleeve, thought the world-weary rock-and-roller. "I didn't want to go *there*," said Margaret defensively. I didn't mean it bad, she thought guiltily. He said he had something to discuss with me, where was I supposed to go? Going to his place would be worse, she argued with herself. She felt bad for wanting to see him. She knew that Adrian wouldn't approve, so she had just not mentioned the appointment to her. But it made Margaret feel even worse that she was looking forward to it so. She was desperate to see Owen. Because there was hope, in her Owen. She thought, he'll know what I should do.

"Well, I don't wanna see Owen, baby. I don't like Owen." Adrian wanted to strike her spaced-out girlfriend. There was no way she could win. How disrespectful, to bring her ex to their house, to their home. We'll have to get away from here, she thought excitedly, a plan forming in her brain, away from all these men. Adrian felt energized; there was nothing more stimulating for her than this kind of challenge. All I need is some cash, and we'll be on our own, out of this cornball world where old men interfere with your family. We'll go away. Just take off, just the two of us, away from them all. She would show them. I'm gonna make so much money, sell so much dope, that they won't be able to touch us, Adrian told herself. "I have business," she said authoritatively. "I have things to do." It would be Margaret and her forever, insulated from the world. "So see fuckin' Owen," she said with a superior smile. Adrian threw some cash on the table and resolutely strode from the restaurant. The only way to beat them is at their own game, Adrian thought, as she enjoyed her own stylish walk.

Margaret was stunned. She was alone, deserted. She tried to fight the fear, but she was frozen. She couldn't move her arms or legs. Her heart pounded like Adrian's drum machine. She listened to it and tried to focus on Owen. He would help her. He could. Her heartbeat re-

minded her of the scientist's beeping machine, alarming
high-pitched beeps warning of the closer and closer dangerous image. She saw Paul from a distance, as he saw him,
her scientist. Looking down at the junkie slowly, slowly
shooting it into his blood. Maybe the scientist needs help
too, thought Margaret. He needs help from the alien
forces. Probably he would go to Owen for help. He knows
that Owen is smart.

"At first the aliens were spotted near places with large
amounts of heroin. Later, we located them specifically in
London, and in these punk circles many more strange
deaths occurred." The large man was finally able to talk
with someone about his "special mission," and his eyes
burned with intensity. What a relief to talk openly to his old
friend without the stigma of his more recent past to influence the digestion of the data he was offering.

Owen glanced at his strange, tall friend. The years had
made the awkward misfit even more unique. When I was a
young man, thought Owen, I was fascinated by these sorts
of characters. The stranger the personality, the more I
wanted to know them, he reminisced. Perhaps that compul-
sion was related to my study of acting, he thought of himself generously. Now he felt guiltily irritated at the inter-
ruption to his daily routine. Not that he didn't believe the
scientist. He had always suspected that UFOs were a real
phenomenon that was being whitewashed by the govern-
ment. It was just inconvenient to have this ex-alumnus person drop by. Whether or not aliens were killing punks was
another story. So many talented people had been wasted by
their drug habits. It was awesome to think about. Owen
thought of his Margaret and started to hurt. He could
hardly believe the transition in his baby, his beauty. Now
she looked like the nasty punks, and occasionally she wore
their dead expression too. And he was excluded. One of the

outsiders, the ones that didn't "get it." It was the first
generation that he didn't empathize with, the first one ever,
after scads of classes, that he didn't understand. What was
behind that "fashion world" gaze? Not ideas, not anything
he could decipher. Only conceit, as though they were the
only ones that had ever felt pain. He hated them. They were
cold, unfeeling, and stupid. But why are there so many of
them, even from privileged homes? Owen broke into a cold
sweat. Maybe I'm getting old, thought Owen. Maybe this is
finally the final generation gap. No, his brain shouted, no.
They're just misled kids, and Margaret is being ruined by
her association with them. He missed her. Even her stub-
born, one-track ways. She'll do this like she does everything, obsessively. I have to stop her, he worried. "Nothing
strange about deaths in punk circles. They kill each other
by shooting too much dope," Owen answered the scientist.

"You interrupted me. Listen to what I have to say. The
most interesting fact we found"—Johann always said "we,"
in case he was having trouble convincing an unenlightened
subject; it sounded more impressive than just "I"—"these
killings occurred during sexual intercourse."

Owen stared at the intense stranger in front of the slide
projector. He had always seemed a stranger, remembered
Owen. But it went deeper than the obvious physical handi-
cap. Even when Johann was in school he was detached.
Even then, he tried to keep people at a distance. Funny,
how people change by becoming more like themselves. By
becoming a scientist, Johann had further insulated himself
from the world. This researcher is as outside the society as
the creatures he studies, thought Owen objectively. Con-
tradicting that is Johann's enthusiasm right now, observed
Owen. Johann seems more animated than I've ever seen
him. What's he got on those slides? What did he just say?
Aliens killing punks during sex? Owen wondered. "You

mean you made slides of sexual intercourse?" queried the teacher.

He doesn't understand the portent of what I am saying, thought Johann nervously. After keeping this secret for all this time, how did I manage to pick such a poor person to reveal it to? Does he think that I'm joking? "It's not funny. We have not only located UFOs, but we have managed to photograph the creature inside of the craft," announced Johann as he watched Owen let down the blinds. Does he think I'm going to show him slides of humans coupling? thinks the scientist fearfully. "I am going to show you documentation of our progress."

Large pink blurbs blasted the walls of Owen's study. In the cool, dark room, the splashes of color comforted Owen. Almost immediately he found his head nodding with fatigue. I didn't sleep much last night, he remembered, thinking of the woman.

"This is the moment when it brings death to a person," said Johann. The slide looked to Owen like a photograph from a laser show. "The state we described as a positive reaction immediately follows this one."

"You think killers are happy after they kill? Even if that's true, you've given the alien human emotions, that's anthropomorphical," said Owen triumphantly. He was pleased that he remembered the term after all the years; then he realized how ridiculous the whole situation was. What am I arguing with him about? thought Owen, irritated. This isn't debating class in college. Johann should be investigating this with someone from the scientific community, if his claim is true. Suddenly everything the scientist said seemed suspiciously unscientific. Johann continued with his relentless polemic. Why is he convincing me? thought Owen. What does he want? Owen looked around in the dark, searching for a clock. As Johann droned on about the UFO,

Owen worried about missing his meeting with Margaret. He was sleepy and afraid he would nod out and miss their appointment.

Last night she had been a middle-aged redhead with a fleshy body and creamy white skin. It wasn't the first woman he had dated since his breakup with Margaret. The evening had been pleasant, the sex exhilarating, but Owen couldn't sleep in the same bed with her. She wasn't an unattractive person, but he felt repulsed by the cuddling. Owen found that disturbing. With most of his girlfriends he had felt affectionate afterward. Lately, with new women, he would fall asleep in an embrace, until the middle of the night. Then he would wake, alarmed, always alarmed, suddenly painfully aware that, whomever he was with, their bodies didn't fit together properly. Alarmed that it wasn't his Margaret pressed to him. They always had slept close, like two puppies. Like one organism. One organism after orgasm, he giggled. Their bodies fit perfectly together. Despite their age difference, being at different stages of their lives, they were the same in their rest. There was something final about the way they slept together. There was always such a pure, deep rest, like none he had ever known.

The sharp pain in her hip made Margaret aware that she hadn't moved. She glanced fervently around the diner, frightened that she had attracted attention to herself by not moving. People will think that I'm crazy or something, to sit so long without moving. She tried to move her left leg. Needles, that's what we called it when we were kids. She wanted to punch her bloodless muscles, like she had as a child, to get the circulation going; but she didn't. If anyone had noticed my lack of movement earlier, they might be questioning my emotional balance, she thought prudently. If they catch me pounding my leg, they'll for sure think I'm loony. The sight of the check on the table in front of her made Margaret even more anxious. I don't remember anyone bringing the check, she thought, panicking. Oh, stop it, she said to herself, no one cares, this is Manhattan, you're just being paranoid. She looked around herself. No one was paying the slightest bit of attention to her, or to the whole front section of the room, for that manner. But still, Margaret could not get over the feeling that someone was watching her. That would be the topping on the cake, she thought to herself, if I started pounding my leg. That's real bag-lady behavior. She picked up the money and check slowly, like bringing together pieces of a puzzle. Adrian had left just enough money to cover the check. Margaret pressed the bills flat over the invoice so that the waitress-person, whoever it was, wouldn't find out that she, or he, had been stiffed until after Margaret left the restaurant.

"I need your help," said the imposing scientist seriously, interrupting Owen's personal thoughts.

My help, thought Owen uncomfortably. Why doesn't he get another scientist involved?

"I cannot get too close because it recognizes me and I am a stranger in this country. There are some problems that are difficult for me to study because of that. I watched the creature from the Empire State Building, but at night it is closed. How can I study the behavior of this creature if 'it' is on private property?"

The creature recognizes him? thought Owen, stifling a smile. He could imagine the easily identifiable enormous German wearing a plastic mask, spying on a flying saucer while in an ineffective disguise. "I don't know," Owen answered, smiling sheepishly. "What do you want me to do about it? I'm just an acting teacher!"

"It seems to me that you don't fully understand what I've been talking about!" Johann replied nervously. "Just now, right now, before I came here, I saw a UFO from the Empire State Building. It was on the roof of an apartment building!"

"I would find it interesting to see it, but I don't see how I can get you into private apartment buildings," Owen stated, staring incredulously at the foreigner. If I was going to get involved in some extracurricular crusade, it would be against nuclear power plants, for nuclear disarmament, or against American intervention in South America. Investigating the UFO threat is not high on my list, thought Owen sarcastically.

Johann's voice got louder with panic. "This alien is killing people."

Owen replied impulsively, "I am not James Bond. Right now I have to meet someone. We'll talk about it later."

The scientist's spirit sagged. Johann knew that the next time he called Owen, Owen would not pick up the receiver after he identified himself to the machine. "You are the only person I know in New York," he said, trying not to plead.

"Call me tomorrow," Owen said warmly. "Keep in touch." He probably believed that he meant it.

Margaret snapped to attention as she became aware that someone was moving toward her from behind. She moved to get out of the restaurant before the person behind her realized that there wasn't enough money for a tip. Her legs were still asleep, but she rose and hobbled from the restaurant. As she pressed on the heavy glass door, the hot air blast and the smell from the street took away her breath. She limped as fast as she could in the oppressive heat, trying to get away from stiffed person in the diner. She hoped that she would be purified by the intense heat. The brightness of the sun hurt her eyes. She played a game where she would close her eyes at intervals to rest them, and try to stay on course and not walk into anyone on the sidewalk. On one such section of "eye-resting," she thought hopefully, Maybe I'll bump into Owen. Then she thought, It's so late, maybe he won't even show. The thought made her open her eyes, and for moment, she thought she saw him in the street. She hurried toward him, then realized the man was far too short. Before her eyes his features changed and it was clear that the man looked nothing like Owen at all. That used to happen to me a lot, she remembered. Before she left college. When they started sleeping together, they would meet secretly, furtively. It was one of the reasons she left college. She was afraid her classmates would find out.

Margaret had felt like one of the crowd, like one of many students at the Manhattan-based college, until she walked into the acting class. He picked her out right away and gave her the best scene to do. Some boys who had been clumsily hitting on her had brought her to the class to impress her. Margaret was impressed, but not by them.

From the beginning he made her feel special. She was lonely, but she didn't know it. It wasn't that she wouldn't have liked to have some friends, it just didn't occur to her to make any. So, it didn't take much for Margaret to be affected. Any attention was refreshing to her. Theirs was a long courtship—no dating, no flowers, no picnics in the grass. There was only that special voice he used when he corrected her, directed her, and the extra time he spent on her scenes. She was as perfect a student as she could be, and he appreciated her enthusiasm. She learned rapidly. She had always been a dreamer, so she could easily imagine being someone else. It was a relief to her to be someone other than herself. He stretched her character range; she stretched her imagination. One day when her acting partner didn't show up, Owen acted a scene with her. It was a subtle moment, easy to miss, that made her aware that he was vulnerable to her as well. During a particularly provocative section of the love scene, Owen blushed.

Suddenly shy Margaret became aggressively flirtatious toward Owen. It was a crusade that the whole class could pick up on. She was embarrassed but couldn't help herself. The young male students who were after her were angry. They couldn't understand why she was after someone older, when she could have one of them. But Owen didn't seem old to her; he seemed younger than her in some ways. The other students made comments, but she didn't think about it. She played it as if she were another character, someone more aggressive, more attractive, more womanly. Soon they were meeting to have sex. When he asked her to join the more professional private classes at night; she quit school. She knew she had won.

Face Fuck

As Margaret wandered home in the heat, she felt guilty for a moment, because of Adrian. That's the worst thing, for the type of person Adrian is, when their girlfriend goes to meet somebody else, thought Margaret. Then she smiled with the irony of it.

When Adrian had arrived on the scene and started to participate in Owen's professional classes, teacher was impressed. Margaret knew that because Owen let Adrian attend classes despite her obvious lack of discipline. He was fascinated by Adrian, even though she always came to class late or early, or sometimes not at all. He couldn't believe that she hadn't had training. Owen didn't believe in "natural" talent. Adrian needed little preparation to give a structured performance, a skill that usually took years to acquire. Of course, she wasn't perfect, but he found her improvisational work and energy level astounding. So, Margaret was fascinated with her too, of course. Because Owen was.

By the time Adrian came into the picture, we had been living together for about a year, thought Margaret. Often Owen had Margaret work with the new students, so he could get a full report. Margaret would tell him how they behaved during the rehearsal period. Still, things hadn't been so good between us at that point, she remembered, Strange that he gave us that scene. Margaret had been sure that Owen saw the way Adrian looked at her. So it seemed strange to her, Margaret was surprised, by the scene Owen gave them. Adrian and Margaret were to work together in a lesbian love scene.

Adrian skipped classes two weeks in a row, so by the time they got to do the scene in the class, Margaret was really ready, certainly prepared. During the private rehearsal, Adrian was astonished that Margaret was so aggressive. After they "rehearsed" for a little while, Adrian got over her surprise. Soon the small woman got control of the situation.

Her feet stopped clopping in the hot haze when Margaret saw Owen standing at the entrance door of her building. For a minute, Margaret thought nothing had changed. That she had just gone to the store and he was waiting to help her bring the packages upstairs, like he used to. He looked so cute. A little uncomfortable for being caught caring, like a kid with his hand in a forbidden cookie jar. But that feeling vanished as soon as she got close. He started staring at her hair, at the evidence of change, and all the disapproving things he had started saying, before Adrian, came to her in a flood. Why do I always only remember the romantic parts? she thought of herself disparagingly. Why can I never remember the negative things about people? They hadn't even spoken yet and already her disappointment was complete.

At the end of their relationship, often Margaret felt she was too flawed to live with him. She never felt that he didn't love her, only that they couldn't live together. Because she did everything wrong. She had started dropping things and forgetting things. The scariest thing she forgot, however, was who she was before Owen. She couldn't remember. Her life had become his.

Owen said, "Hi, baby." And instantly Margaret was—his baby. His for the saying of it. She tried to fight it, but it was hot, and she was tired. "Come upstairs," she said softly, and they walked in silence. He had taught her so much, all that he could, all that she could hold, that somehow she felt he owned a part of her. She couldn't be who she was if not for him. She had tried to fight this obligation, to live like a real couple, but he hadn't wanted it. He didn't want her to change, didn't like her new ideas, ways, suggestions. It seemed to make him nervous, that she should grow—get older, like him. So she kept silent now. Because he needed to know it all. Because she needed him to know.

As they rode in the elevator he reached to twirl her hair around his finger. It was just an old habit he'd developed. Some people chew their fingernails; Owen wrapped strands of Margaret's hair on his fingers. But there wasn't any hair there. It was a subtle action, the withdrawal of his hand, but they both cringed.

Adrian had come on time to the next class. Owen praised Adrian's "interesting" work. It was his pattern to praise the new students, let them gain confidence and get used to the class, then gently begin to constructively criticize their work. Owen was a master at marrying the positive with the negative so artfully that the students didn't even know they were being criticized. But Adrian knew. After a few classes she sensed the transition in his technique. She didn't fight it. But nobody could tell Adrian what to do. As soon as Owen started to teach her, she stopped coming to class. But Adrian came to the party.

As with all the parties that Owen had thrown in the acting studio, the size was out of hand. But Margaret never suspected that this would happen. Owen and his male friends, people he had known for years, had decided to throw a party. Margaret was eager to help, eager to lend her energies to the task. But the reality of the mess, the crowd, and that she was the only one working, was all too evident. They came in and out by the hundreds. Everyone except Margaret was having a good time. As soon as Adrian arrived she made a beeline for the kitchen. She found what she expected to find—Margaret with her hands in the sink, frantic, trying to keep some order in the chaos. Adrian's suggestion that Margaret was being unfairly exploited, catering a party she didn't throw, came as a complete surprise to Margaret. When she tried on Adrian's idea, the flood of anger and humiliation that Margaret felt, of course, had to be rectified. And of course, Adrian had the perfect solution: that they should leave together, leave the party and let Owen find another unpaid laborer. Margaret had never done anything like it in her life. She had always been a "good" girl; done the "right" thing. But if he had only checked on her once during the horrific evening, she would have forgiven him. It seemed right, this small revenge. If she was going to be treated like she wasn't part of the party, she wouldn't be. She wouldn't be part of his party. Anyway, he wasn't even paying attention to her.

Now, of course, Margaret understood why Adrian had been so good in acting class. Adrian was always acting, not only when she was onstage. She was always in the spotlight, always in a dramatic situation. And now Margaret was included, since her dive into Club life. It was constant theater, in and out of the apartment. But Margaret wasn't going to explain it to Owen. She wasn't even going to tell him. She would keep her insight to herself. He wasn't one of them. Anyway, he didn't want information from her lips. Her lips, in his mind, were only for kissing.

As soon as they got into the apartment, Margaret went out to the roof. She wanted to be as far away from the bed as possible. She didn't want him to get any ideas. So, even though it was hot and bright, she moved all her tools, paints, accessories, jewelry out to the roof and pretended to be involved in her plans for a fashion shoot. She wanted him to see that she was doing good, living a creative life. Subconsciously she needed him to approve. If he would only say something nice to her, like he used to, then she would know that she was all right.

So, they settled outdoors, on a roof in the Manhattan sky, under the Empire State Building. He busied himself by rolling a joint; she changed her clothes. Changing her clothes was something Margaret did often in public, most of her friends did. Models were always taking off clothes and putting clothes on in large public rooms. It was no big deal. But Margaret felt uncomfortable now, because he was rolling a joint. It disturbed Margaret. She didn't want him to think she was provoking him. It was Owen's habit to smoke pot before football games, foreign films, and sex. But Margaret didn't own a television.

Before Margaret had lived with Owen, she had always believed that if two people loved each other enough, they could work out anything—that it would be all right. It came as such a shock to her, to her whole belief system, when it didn't work out. When it became clear that he only wanted certain parts of her, that the other parts irritated him. Because she knew that he loved her. She was sure of that. That was why it was so sad. Because love wasn't enough.

Knowing that didn't change that she needed him now. Margaret needed very much to believe in something, even if it wasn't for long, wasn't to last. Margaret needed to know that he cared about her.

"Everything you've done since you left me is very self-destructive. What I'm telling you is for your own good. Adrian is a bad influence. You're not yourself. She doesn't care anything about you. She's only using you. You're ruining your future, your career."

The barrage of disapproval made her desperate. Automatically, she started to flirt in spite of her fear. The fear of what it would lead to. She wasn't consciously aware of the change. It was subtle. It was her way to get the attention she needed; the only way to stop his "concerned" criticism. After all, it had always worked before. She needed his approval. Being sexually desired was what made her feel valuable. But she was confused; she felt guilty using this power.

Because she had long ago sworn off that. When she cut her hair, she decided not to do it anymore. Discrepancies in her own behavior always made her feel uncomfortable. So she defended herself verbally as well, making sure that Owen was aware that she wasn't like before. That they were different; different age groups, different cultures, different sides of the world. But there was another reason for pointing out that the situation had changed. She needed to remind herself not to be too romantic, not to forget that time had changed everything. She needed to remember that love isn't the answer. Because Margaret could not hold another disappointment or disillusionment in her heavy heart.

"What are you talking about? It's the only thing I care about, my career. What do you think I'm doing right now?

I'm getting ready to shoot with a fashion photographer, who I met at the Club, who's going to come here and . . ." Her voice trailed off because Owen touched her and started to speak. He held her body above the elbows and looked into her face, concerned, reprimanding her gently, as though she were a small child.

"He really only wants to sleep with you," he said. The way she dresses, it's no wonder he wants to come to her apartment, thought Owen as he examined her form in the bright, revealing costume.

Margaret pulled free and started to apply red, white, and black color to her angled face. It seemed funny to her that he didn't understand so much. "Nobody fucks from the Club. Everybody is gay." She painted a line on her chin. She suddenly felt sorry there was such a wide gap between them. "It's you that thinks about fucking all the time," said Margaret, smiling at him, her bright eyes closing the chasm.

"And your vocabulary has been reduced to two words—fuck and shit." Owen smiled as he said it. The parental tone in his voice was missing. The whole situation seemed ludicrous to him. But Margaret didn't comprehend that. She pressed on, defending her style, justifying her life.

"What do you mean? I should say 'making love' instead of fucking? 'Making love' is a sixties expression. Now it's the nineteen eighties. I don't know what the rest of the world likes, but I like to fuck."

Margaret knew she wasn't being clear enough, that she was failing to explain. As if it would make it clearer, she put on her lowest, loudest outfit and said provocatively, "Is that better? What do you think, Professor?"

Owen took a long drag on the thin joint and looked her over. "You look like a hooker. And you act like a hooker. You're going to end up in the hospital with some horrible sexual disease." Margaret's giggle caused Owen to laugh at his own amusing deduction. The mental image of the large, miniskirted Margaret, complete with red headdress, lying in St. Vincent's with the clap seemed as ludicrous as his parental role in her life. In spite of all his years of life, Owen still felt as though he hadn't learned anything. He drew on the joint. It seemed as if wisdom was the unraveling of everything he had imagined he knew. That he would stand in judgment of someone else's life and lend advice was a task far, far away from him. He felt like skipping, riding his bike to his friend's house, or going on an adventure in the backlots of MGM. It took all his available discipline to pull his mind back to his professor regimen. He wondered if Margaret had sensed his temporary lapse into his past. She continued the dialogue and he knew she hadn't caught him. But sometimes he was sure that she had gone back in time with him. After and before orgasm, in an emotional thrall, they had been children together, lovers and children. It hurt him to think that she wouldn't play with him there again.

"You don't understand anything," Margaret said with sad eyes. "So I look like a hooker. So what?" It's as much the truth as wearing an apron, or a prettily sweet dress. To be dressed overly sexy is a more direct way. It's better, she agonized. Finding the right words for the feelings that evoked her flamboyant dress was difficult for her. She knew why only in her heart. She tried her best, But her mouth wouldn't cooperate and help her to get her ideas verbal and clear. "You like it. I can see that you want me. So why do you live these lies?" In some strange way Margaret felt she was protecting herself by dressing provocatively. "The way you want me to dress and behave is as a sweet housewife, slave of her husband's will. A hooker is at least independent. I'm nobody's victim. I choose. It's only fair that I warn them, this pussy has teeth. I want to show them that I'm aware of what's going down."

Poor Margaret, she didn't know that the reason she felt protected when she dressed like a whore had to do with her own soft heart. If she made it clear that she wasn't going to care for those she slept with, the role secured her from caring herself. It had to be that much of a cartoon so that she felt she had the right to be cold, or angry. But to fuck with someone she wasn't going to care about, this had to be very clear, because she couldn't keep this separation without a visual aid. The separation between herself and the world was too unclear.

"Since you cut your hair you look like a dyke," said Owen in his best teacher voice. He tried to hide his anger with reason. After all the work they had done, she was at the perfect age, she had been the perfect type, success had been only a matter of time. The casting directors, once aware of her skills, would have loved this natural beauty. Now all was lost. No one would hire this freak show of colors for a role. She was hidden from them.

"That's my choice as well," said Margaret. He thinks Adrian made me cut my hair, she thought, outraged. The one thing I really do all by myself and Adrian gets the credit for it. The way I look is political. I'm not for sale. I don't want to look the way they like. Owen thinks I should dress for everyone but myself. To look like his ideal. He really only cares about himself or he could understand how I feel, thought Margaret painfully. She almost screamed, "Nobody can tell me that I'm just a woman."

"You were my best student. I invested a lot of time in you," Owen retorted sadly.

Margaret thought, That's all I am to him, a good product, his best result. As though our whole relationship was only incidental. "What are you saying? We spent most of our time in bed." She tried not to remember all the places they went, the comfort they shared, all without words. "Anytime I would try to say anything you would preach to me," whined Margaret.

It hurt that she thought so little of the knowledge he gave her. He felt suddenly violently jealous of whatever Margaret and Adrian shared. That she should listen to Adrian instead of him was the cruelest of jokes. Because that was the first generation he couldn't understand or empathize with. It was the evidence of his age.

"You *should* listen to me, not to Adrian. Adrian has turned you into a real mean bitch. Everyone says it. Try to be sweet." He looked at her with hurt eyes. "You said I didn't teach you anything."

"I didn't say that," said a surprised Margaret. "You taught me a lot." No one could say that Owen hadn't taught her anything, not even Adrian. Margaret wondered where he got that idea. But she knew where he got the other ones. She could imagine his cronies sitting around assuring Owen that he was better off without her. Sure, thought Margaret, I am bitchy to them. I do a real good mean now, but I never did like them really. Now I just don't pretend to. Margaret never could relate to his friends. They seemed to reinforce the worst kind of male mentality in Owen. Whenever she ran into them now, on the street or wherever, Margaret got great pleasure from snubbing them, or saying devastating things, if she could think of any. It was one of the few pleasures of being a "punk," as they would call her. Margaret would call it being honest.

Margaret climbed on the table, strutted in her high shoes. She tried some beads on, then some feathers. She practiced her model walk, and found some comfort in her preening. She found a feather, and paused to put it in her hair. Owen said, "You could have been a star."

He looked at her with such sad eyes. Margaret got angry that he cared so much more for her future than he had for theirs. "Who wants to be a star?" she said. She thought, He sees me as a showcase for his talents as a teacher.

As Owen smoked his joint he watched Margaret watching herself in the mirrors. She seemed to have forgotten his presence in her passion for her own appearance. He gazed into the reflective plastic on which she was dancing. The swirling patterns of color reminded him of the Mardi Gras. Like the circus, he thought for a moment, enjoying the bright moving colors. No, he reconsidered, watching her absorbed in her costumes. People are invited to share enjoyment in the Mardi Gras, or in the circus. These punks not only do not let others enjoy the way they look; they don't enjoy it themselves. They have a fashion-world mentality, he concluded. But Margaret seems so absorbed in her weird clothes. Does she really think she is making art by dressing strange? he thought, concerned suddenly with her rationale. "Why do you present yourself in that way?" he asked, his voice purposely casual. "A real artist would never dress in the style of a trendy group trying to act like hoodlums and hookers."

She had been moving busily in the oppressive heat, trying to lose herself in her daily clothes changing. The sun was biting her exposed skin. She wanted to remove the oppressive corset and change again into something more protective against the ultra-violet rays. But he was watching her so closely, it would be construed as a provocation. "I would be frightened to go out late dressed as a bourgeois. If I dress like this nobody bothers me. They know I have a knife in my pocket and no money."

If she goes out at night looking like that, everyone will assume she's a hooker and try to pick her up, thinks Owen anxiously. "If you carry a knife, someone will use it on you.

I'm telling you this for your own good," says Owen patiently. "All your weird costumes, knives are just for participation in some phony theater."

Margaret was angry at herself for being affected by the concern in his voice. When she had been with him, Margaret had felt protected. Even if it was very animal, him wanting to protect the source of his pleasure; at least she wasn't frightened all the time. Only of him sometimes, not of others. And she was lonely. There is such comfort in being a couple, she thought longingly, even if it's fake. It took all her resolve to try to focus on some feminist thoughts. But still, she couldn't think of anything to help her. After all the literature she had read, the only book about sex roles she could remember was one Owen had had lying around. It had glamorized the man's instinct to protect and control his mate and children. Maybe it is the natural thing, thought Margaret, discouraged. After all, he didn't have me read it. It was I that found it and found it unsettling. I felt that book in my bowels. Then, luckily, she remembered the author's face on the back cover. It was the face of a smug, righteous, old white male. It was what saved her from depression the last time. For all the author's emphasis on might being right, the stronger male winning the best woman, and the advancement of the gene pool, in any other culture the man would have long before been dead of natural causes. She held on to the image of his offensive right-wing face, pulled herself together, and answered Owen. "Are you saying that your blue jeans weren't theater?" she said softly.

She cannot compare this weird cult thing to the sixties rebellion, thought Owen, annoyed. "It's not the same thing," he replied confidently.

He dismissed what I said; it wasn't clear enough, thought Margaret anxiously. No one ever understands what I say.

Because there's something wrong with me, my head is not properly attached to my mouth. That's why I should stay with my own group. We never really talk, but it's supposed to be like that, words don't help. If there are no words, there are no lies. Because everyone is alone. Man is born alone. I'm different and I should stay where I belong, with all the other glamorous freaks. "So your professor wore a three-piece suit and blamed you for your jeans. For him your jeans were too much. And he didn't understand that his suit was also theater. You thought your jeans stood for love, freedom, and sexual equality. We at least know that we're wearing costumes." He didn't seem react to what she said, he only stared at Margaret with a blank face. She looked at him, sad for the vast difference between them that even language could not cross. There's just something wrong with me. I should just accept it and stop trying for the unattainable. Relieved, she stopped feeling anxious and awarded herself a moment of peace. Anyway, it doesn't matter, she told herself unemotionally. He's not one of us.

Owen hadn't meant to imply that he was from the generation of rebellion, it had just happened that way one day in the course of the conversation. That she hadn't noticed that he was obviously too old to be a sixties flowerchild, and that he didn't correct her now, was what froze him. He was humiliated by his own behavior. After living all these years, to stoop to deny them, after earning them, that was inexcusable. It was behavior he would have criticized in someone else when he was a younger man. But, then again, like Margaret, he probably wouldn't have noticed any discrepancy. That's the privilege only of the young, he thought bitterly, to not notice the ravages of time. How young she is, how young and how foolish. Why won't she take some of this knowledge I've earned. I'm a teacher. What's the point of living if no one uses what I've known. "It's self-destructive," he said authoritatively; not because he thought she would listen—she'd heard it often before—but because he didn't know what else to say. And he wanted to help her.

Margaret was upset with herself for speaking out in such a stupid way. None of the ones she knew would have used the label "we." It was just not done. The whole point was not to get pegged as a group. They were all unique, the ones she knew, artists in their own way. She would be mortified if any one of them knew she had talked like that. I should keep my mouth shut, she scolded herself. It's hopeless to try to explain. Everyone who needs to understand already does, without talk. Words distort the truth. They should only be used to dramatic advantage, she reminded herself. Margaret looked at the man before her, who had been her friend until the moment before. She felt isolated. He couldn't hurt her now. So what if she was self-destructive? At least she was trying to find a new way to live instead of making the same mistakes over and over. He seemed a very sad figure to her suddenly, trapped in his own holding pattern. "Maybe." she said sadly. "But you're self-destructive too." What could he possibly get from her, why was he there? She had nothing to offer him but sad stories and broken dreams. "Or else why would you be here?" she asked, defeated. He should go back where he belongs and leave me here, she decided. "We at least have fun while we destroy ourselves. You are boring," Margaret said flippantly.

Immediately she felt bad for saying it and grabbed the reflective plastic in frustration. It rattled loudly as she pulled it off the long runway table. Furtively she tried to get away from her guilt by throwing herself into the racket she was making. She dragged the noisy mirrored cover into the apartment and placed it over the bright striped rug on the floor. The reflective surface threw bits of colored light all over the cool, darkened interior. This will look even better at night when the colors from the neon signs are even more intense, she decided happily. After arranging her own appearance, next she worked on the apartment. It was her pursuit of routine and it soothed her to believe she had some order in her life.

Owen followed her into the apartment and closed the roof door behind him. Again, she was involved in some absorbing creative activity; this time it looked suspiciously like interior decorating. He couldn't help but be amused by it. The light, as she bent over in her miniskirt, reflected up off the material she was manipulating and bounced off her tender white skin. In the high shoes, which appeared to extend her legs, she reminded him of a skittish thoroughbred colt. What an amazing creature, he thought, watching her brightly clad form. What a woman, he observed, as he noted the way the red crest in her hair bounced as she moved about the room. Who would guess that I would ever come to know a girl like this?

Never look back, Margaret told herself. Don't try to understand the why's; life has no reasons. She tried to fight the bad feeling she had from telling Owen he was boring. He *is* boring, she instructed herself. But it didn't help. How could I be so mean to him? she punished herself. Why would I hurt Owen? He's only been good to me. I'm just no good, she thought, as she looked helplessly around the apartment, searching for distractions. I'm just a slimy old slug with no will of my own. She was already missing him. Fear also governed her indecisiveness. She was feeling so uncentered that just being in the room with Owen panicked her. It had happened before that he told her what she thought, and she thought it. It was so easy to lose herself in his ideal of what a woman should be. That was something she knew how to be: the best woman. The role was seductive and familiar. And Owen had been smoking that pot.

Suddenly, he was pressing himself to her, his front to her back. He held her close, his palms pressing into her belly, pulling them together so she could feel him swelling. It was his way, to appear suddenly from behind. Margaret was filled with fear; it reminded her of the other one. Owen couldn't know how it frightened her, she decided, her heart racing. She only wished that she could control herself enough not to blurt out what had happened there. It would only make him angry, if he knew, if she told him about the guy with the pills. Then he would attack her lifestyle and tell her what to do. She felt so fragile that another critical word would be too much to take.

It is truly amazing how quickly she excites me, thinks Owen happily. She feels so good, he muses, as his hands travel up into even softer crevices and crannies. He feels her tremble and wonders at her sensitivity. Does she realize how excited I get over her timidity? he marvels. She must, he decides. It was the overwhelming wonder of our sexual life together that her coyness made me so hard, so fast.

His fingers traveled over her sunburned flesh, and Margaret was proud of her self-control. At least I manage to keep my mouth shut over this, she thought proudly, as she suppressed her cry of pain. She had to hide that she had been sweltering in the sun. He would know that she had been avoiding him if she complained about her sunburn. It was her own fault. She shouldn't have invited him there if she didn't want to have sex with him. He would want to know why not. She was afraid to tell him. But it wasn't only fear of his anger over her way of life that prohibited her telling him. Instinctively she thought not to let him know her fear. She was certain that he would find it all the more titillating. That was all she knew to hang on to, that they should not know her fear. It was her way of protecting herself. Margaret remembered the earlier man who could smell "it." Had it not been for Adrian . . . She shuddered at the thought, and Owen pressed tighter against her. "Oh, you want me now, huh?" she uttered quietly. She was so very tired.

"You have the best legs," Owen joked. "We both have good legs. If we had children they would have the best legs to stand on." It was their joke. He knew it would cheer her up, but hadn't bargained on being so affected himself. They both had tears in their eyes as they laughed.

He always said that silly joke when he wanted to charm her; and it always worked. Silly, sweet, Owen, she thought fondly. He doesn't want to harm me. Why not just let him do it, she considered. Then she remembered all the hurtful things he had said before. She wanted so to believe that he cared for her, but he said such awful things. "I thought I looked ugly and would give you diseases," whined Margaret sarcastically.

"Come here," said Owen, smiling. She pouts like a child, he thought, charmed by her vulnerability. His hand slipped between her legs, and he was surprised at how ready she seemed. He had been holding off, waiting for her to get as excited as he was. He prided himself on not rushing women. Owen wondered at Margaret's attitude about sex. It's always the same, he thought. She acts like she doesn't know if she wants to, but she never says no. Poor thing seems ashamed by her own desires. He found it exciting that she didn't have control of her own passion. She trembles, he thought amorously, and doesn't know what to do about her own excitement. She needs a man to guide her through the act; her own desire confuses her.

"Don't," Margaret pleaded as she pushed Owen's hand from between her wet legs. She was sweating profusely and was nervous about what to do. She was afraid. What if I got some disease from the creep from before, I don't want to give it to Owen. But she couldn't tell him why not. "Not today," she said timidly. It was hard for Margaret to reject him, because she needed to be held. Margaret wanted to be liked, and her voice carried her conflict.

She's so sexy, so feminine, he thought, holding her trembling body. Even her own passion frightens her. He smiled. "You don't know what you want," he said, charmed by her fragility.

"No," she replied angrily. "And you do? Who do you want? Me?" Margaret was so frustrated. She didn't know what to do. I should just let him do it, that's what he deserves, she thought viciously, and was surprised by her own anger. She had never thought mean things about Owen before. Before, when he had disappointed her, she had just left. But now she was gloating over the idea that she could give him the clap. She felt his hand slipping between her legs again. Here we go again, she thought sarcastically, he's going to find a little sweat down there to justify mauling me.

"You're all wet," said Owen knowingly. He was getting impatient. It was hard not to feel rejected when she needed so much convincing. Getting Margaret past the petting stage has always been difficult, he reassured himself. Once we get started, she'll warm up.

They're all the same, she was thinking. Men can't control themselves. When they're excited they think with their penis. It serves him right if I give him a disease. Owen squeezed Margaret and pulled her gently to the bed. As her buttocks touched the bedspread, she panicked. Margaret had a memory that made her hide her face in Owen's arms. For a moment, Vincent was hitting her. It was the moment when she realized she was in trouble. He's not like them,

Margaret thought desperately. I'm thinking all those terrible things to Owen because of last night, she reasoned. Owen is good. He doesn't want to hurt me, she thought helplessly.

It was then that Owen started to sing. " 'You'd be so easy to hug . . . So nice to be kissing all others above . . .' " It was one of those old, corny songs again. He sang them all the time when they were together. Margaret had never heard most of them before Owen. They were so sentimental, she had often thought that they wouldn't even apply to her grandparents' relationship. But they worked on her. She didn't know why. Maybe it was because Owen sang so hopelessly off-key, a fact that he was well aware of, and still sang for her. " 'So right to keep the home fires burning for . . . So great that I can't help yearning for . . . We wouldn't get wet in the rain, So happy together that it's really a shame . . . That you can't see, your place with me . . . You'd be so easy to hug.' " By the end of the song, Margaret was mush. That he would sit there groping for the words of the corny song with Margaret in his arms, sporting his gigantic (it seemed to Margaret) hard-on without complaint; was proof enough to her that he loved her. After all, everyone knows that if the penis is hard for so long without relief, it starts to hurt. That's what the boys had all told her.

Owen was surprised, when he entered her, that Margaret was so tight. He felt a little strange about her acquiescence. Not because she had been so docile when he stroked her to get her aroused—she had always been shy about her own pleasure—but because her concentration seemed to be somewhere else. He held off from his orgasm more than once, when he caught her looking out the window. Owen even tried to figure out what she was looking at out there, while he was fucking her. He was pretty amused with himself about that bit of maneuvering. He was reassured, however, that she was enjoying herself. Because occasionally, just when he thought he had lost her attention, she would get all crazy in the eyes and cry out, not scream really, like she was coming, but make a furtive animal sound nonetheless. It seemed to take forever. But the heat of the room, coupled with the high humidity, made for slippery, sleazy sex; the kind he remembered from when he was a young man. And he was not going to come without her. Owen was proud that he could hold his own in sex as well as any young stud.

As soon as Owen had inserted it in her, Margaret remembered the pain. Even with the Quaaludes it had hurt. She just didn't remember it until she was reminded. By blocking out the memory, she had protected herself from the horror of being taken against her will. Her forehead was being banged against the marble wall, a cold step digging into her stomach, her smell of his mouth as he tried to force his tongue to hers. And then there would be Owen, pulling her chin up so she was facing him. She knew he only wanted to see her, to see her eyes, but she couldn't help it, she got them mixed up. It made her wild with sadistic pleasure when she imagined he was catching her disease, that it would infect his penis and he would get open, gory sores. Then, there would be moments of clarity, sweet objective peace. In these moments Margaret's thoughts would wander to other subjects. To her alien scientist alone in Manhattan, carrying his large instrument in the strange black valise.

Johann Hoffmann stood on the curb looking straight up at the chosen building in front of him. It will have to be above the lip of the adjoining building, he said to himself in German as he traced an imaginary line between the two structures. Anyone seeing him on the street, thought Margaret, would think him a zealous tourist, studying the architecture of Manhattan skyscrapers. In a short time, without knowing the area, the scientist had figured out which building held the alien, and which building was best to study "it" from. As he walked to the entrance to the chosen building, again he checked the juxtaposition of it to the other structure, just to enjoy his progress. Now, all that I have to accomplish, he reminded himself, is to gain access to one of these apartments facing west in this building. But as he examined the intercom, Johann Hoffmann was dismayed to find that the names beside the buzzers had no numbers. How will I know which person has visual access? he said to himself, perplexed. It was then that the woman appeared.

I've bought myself flowers and it still hasn't helped, thought Sylvia grimly as she exited the cab across from her apartment building. She had tried to plan her evening with enthusiasm, but too many nights of television and take-out made this night seem like another lonely chore. In her mind she anticipated selecting a vase for the thirsty flowers in her hand while crossing the busy intersection. Shall I choose this one or that one? she mused, trying to entertain herself as she walked across the street. It's no use, she then thought, exasperated, I might as well give in and be miserable. And then she saw the large man.

He was standing in her foyer, looking at all the intercom labels with great concern. As Sylvia entered the lobby, she asked assertively, "May I help you?"

"What side of the building do your windows face?" asked the scientist earnestly. His smile came as an afterthought and Johann hoped she didn't notice his bad manners.

Sylvia was nonplussed. What a strange question, she thought. That's the most unusual come-on I've ever heard. Even though it was Friday afternoon, and hardly the schedule for a city official's visit, Sylvia replied with a wry smile,

"Are you the Fire Inspector?" She was thinking of her own personal fire and her own personal amusement.

Johann was not used to women. He was certainly not used to women who stared directly into his face. For a moment, he was rattled by the aggressive American. "No," he answered bashfully. "I am a scientist."

Sylvia did not notice the subtle signs of his discomfort, his lowered eyes and quiet voice. Normally Johann spoke with a booming timbre; his co-workers would regularly ask him to lower his voice. But Sylvia had no way of knowing that. His whisper sounded like a regular voice level to her. "Well," she said, confidently continuing her joke, "I put my fire extinguisher in and my exits are all accessible."

It wasn't often that a woman flirted with the giant man. When Johann figured out that he was being entertained, a large smile (his head being so large, his smile would have to be) broke out over his tired face. "I am a scientist," he repeated, as a matter of introduction. His impulse was to kiss her hand, but he refrained, being unsure of American customs and certainly inexperienced with women.

"Are you studying windows?" Sylvia remarked, half joking but righteously suspicious. His awkwardness provoked her to wonder if he was damaged, if he would qualify for her particular needs.

Herr Hoffmann had dealt with enough customs officials to recognize a disrespectful mistrust adroitly. He remained calm, in spite of the wail of internal sirens, and explained in the most general terms his foreign lips would form. He knew if he explained too much his errand would never be completed, and the questioning would continue relentlessly. "Windows have something to do with my research," he began quietly. "You see, I am an astrophysicist and I am researching some phenomenon which has occurred in some countries. I am from West Berlin. I will show you my identification . . ." He reached for his wallet, and paused to choose his next words. Johann was sickened by the hopelessness he felt; he knew his chances of gaining entry to the building were not great.

Johann's anxiety was wasted on Sylvia. Sylvia had not heard a word of his explanation. She had been absorbed in scrutinizing the scientist's manner and dress. Titillated by his foreign tongue and European clothing, she thought excitedly, Of course they dress more low-key than Americans are given to believe. The promotion of European designers warrants the selling of the idea that Europeans are these fabulous dressers that we should emulate; but it's not the look of their clothes that's so different. Sylvia longed to caress the textures of his clothing. The fabrics seemed to cry out "Touch me" to her. Of course, she found it edifying, this exposure to another culture, but what fascinated her, on the most basic level, was his size. His giant-ness has a downtrodden elegance to it, she decided. It's time for an American to teach him how to enjoy being large, she leched, not without humor, as Johann held out his ID, waiting to be examined. "Have you had dinner?" asked the woman producer with smoke in her eyes.

Johann Hoffmann was without words for a moment. He was so surprised he didn't know what to say. Quickly he said, "No!?!" not wanting to spoil his chance for access to the building. As Sylvia replied, relief flowed into his tense body.

"You know," she cooed, "I have free evening. Why don't you explain everything to me over dinner?" He looked at a loss for words. Sylvia didn't want to lose him, so she eagerly urged him, "Come on, let's go upstairs."

It's so wet, thought Margaret, when Owen's gyrations distracted her from weaving her inner monologue. Their sweat had made a salty pond of the immediate area. Margaret imagined herself floating on a river, with her guardian scientist watching . . . No! she panicked. He can't gain access to watch me. It's not him who watches, Margaret told herself. He couldn't even get Owen to help. It's the one he watches who watches me, she thought, pleased with her own importance. And he, no, "it," is more powerful than anything mortal. "It" is the light of stars, pure energy. And "It" watches this man on me.

Sylvia was pleased. She was pleased with herself, for she had achieved her objective. The large man was ambling throughout her apartment, Checking it out, as they say. At first, she was a little disconcerted over his compulsive behavior; he literally jumped to the front room of her domain before she could even get her jacket off. But then she remembered her own trip to the other continent, and the feeling of being displaced. Of course, she said to herself, it's important to him to get his bearings to understand his locale in this strange city. He's a foreigner here, and most likely a little anxious about losing his sense of direction. That insight made her feel good about herself. She felt feminine for being so understanding, for not being judgmental. I *can* put aside my office behavior, she told herself proudly.

Johann Hoffmann was feeling very proud of himself as well. Without the use of his special equipment, he could see with his naked eye the sun reflecting off the alien craft. It had landed among the debris on the roof of the apartment where the scientist had first spotted the junkie. As he gazed at the shiny object, Johann Hoffmann mused. Inside that strange metal disk, he said pompously to himself, is the future. And I have found the most appropriate window in all of New York City from which to carry out this important research. Now, what I have to do is convince this attractive woman to let me have access and not let myself get distracted from this glorious task. He looked again. Johann could barely make out someone moving in one of the brightly decorated windows. He found himself compelled to do extensive research on the people who attracted the alien as well. The foreigner was overwhelmed by curiosity. The scientist was eager to begin his work. "It's the perfect spot for watching," he called to Sylvia, testing the water. When he didn't hear a response, Johann peeked around the corner, to find Sylvia on the telephone.

In her eagerness to plan the evening, Sylvia had presumptuously acted on her scheme. She was embarrassed when the large man caught her on the phone ordering Chinese without consulting him. Because I'm so used to taking charge, I neglected to think about his authority being threatened, Sylvia punished herself. He'll find me unattractive, she worried. "I'm ordering Chinese, is that all right with you?" she said timidly. She was frightened he would find her too overpowering and not want to be with her anymore.

The scientist stood between Sylvia and his cherished window, still gloating over the discovered treasure. The woman mentioned something to him about food, but his mind was on more important matters. He still couldn't believe his luck. "It's perfect. It's perfect," he said, needing to share his happiness. But he couldn't take his eyes off his favorite spot, Sylvia's window.

What a relief! thought Sylvia happily. He's not threatened by a woman who makes decisions. He said it's perfect, and it is! It leaves me free to get acquainted and not have to bother with cooking. It's a good choice and he appreciates it. What more could a woman want? she thought, appreciating his anatomy. He's probably just as liberated in his sexual practices. "This is Sylvia," she said, loud enough for him to hear (just in case he forgot her name), and in response to the garbled voice on the line. "Yes," she answered, looking at the scientist. "I'd like two orders of shrimp fried Rice, an order of shrimp with lobster sauce and an order of shrimp with pea pods. Yes. The same address," she said automatically, while admiring his physique.

Johann Hoffmann had never experienced a woman staring openly at his body before. He had no idea how to handle it. The scientist wasn't even sure if it was a mating ritual, so he ignored it, and gave notice to the decor. There was a baby grand piano in the apartment, many books, and many plants. He knew that women appreciate comments about their homes, but he didn't know what to say. Johann rarely gave any time to considering his own comfort, let alone the aesthetics of furniture arrangement. He wondered how someone could waste the time, for example, to hang so many pictures in one unit. On closer examination, Johann noticed they were posters, most from older movie promotions. It was then that he saw the image of the alien craft. A much more fantastic rendition than the real thing, he noted, but a UFO nonetheless. "That's what I'm working on!" he said, astounded, staring at the huge poster.

"That's what *I'm* working on," said Sylvia, relieved. She had long ago finished her phone call and had been waiting for him to put some effort into making conversation. Finally! she thought when he found something in common that they could discuss.

"Are you a researcher?" queried the confused scientist.

"No. I am a television producer," responded Sylvia proudly. "Do you think that they really exist?" she said in an overly feminine manner.

Thank God they do, thought Margaret, racked with pain. She was so sore from his constant movement that tears were rolling uncontrollably down her warm cheeks. I hate him! she would think, wild with rage and pain, and then check herself, understanding her anger was misplaced. Boy! am I lucky to have the interest of this alien. "It" is watching me, studying *me*, It won't let Owen kill me, she reassured herself, deluded with pain. If "It" could have seen the other one, it would have killed him. Killed him dead. Too bad he couldn't see me on the stairs. It came here looking for heroin, but It found something better. The alien found me. He's watching me. Her pain subsided and Margaret found herself aroused. She was hot. Wet with pleasure, the pleasure of being studied, observed, scrutinized by her bodyless lover. Pure color, pure energy, her alien was a contained fusion beyond the animal state of being human. He watches me through the mirrors, she mused. He was above her on the roof, but he could see her reflection through the mirrors which collected her. Collected her image and projected it outside to the roof, to her roof where he—It watched. He is sending his beams through the mirror, and they're touching me. This explosive lumination from beyond the stars is touching me. Its light is caressing me, touching me, calling me. She was frenzied with excitement. Margaret knew that It wanted her to be his, and his alone. Owen's movements, which had seemed overwhelming to her, suddenly seemed pathetic next to the stimulation her alien was providing. Margaret was so excited, she thought Owen was trying some new maneuver when he had the spasms. They had a pleasing rhythmic pattern to them. Margaret had never felt so alive with passion. As she realized the alien was killing Owen, she started to come. It wants me, she realized with joy and ecstasy. It's claiming me as his alone, she thought. And she saw the crystal shooting down the beam. She saw it enter Owen's scalp and she knew it was sucking him, using him, sucking out the juice; and she experienced an orgasm like she had never known before. Her body quaked with pleasure as she knew It was killing him. And by killing him, It was making her his. His for all time. Her body opened and closed, opened and closed in waves that seemed to go on forever. When it stopped, and she was spent, Margaret pulled the glass, the slice of crystal from Owen's head, in an aroused, romantic stupor. As she held it, the perfectly beautiful arrow, it disappeared before her eyes.

Margaret was happy. She wandered the apartment in a stumbling stupor of happiness. For the first time she knew peace. Now, I am really and truly loved, she told herself. And she kneeled before the door to her roof, awed by Its presence, and the show of his love for her. But I shouldn't go out on the roof, she warned herself. Because it might hurt his—I mean, Its—feelings to understand that It's not well hidden there. Even the scientist can see him—no—Its —craft without telescopic equipment. If he knows, I know It's there, It might be upset and fly away. He might leave. Leave me here alone, she thought, frightened, too frightened to move. After a while she got up off her knees. She didn't mind the pain of staying in the same position. The rug was pressing a pattern into her knees and the tops of her feet were cramped, but she didn't want It to see any ugly marks on her legs. So Margaret rose from her shrine, arranged her red knees, but continued to stand in awe, in the open doorway to her roof. She thought that any sudden movement might make the UFO fly away. Or, that the UFO might feel more secure if It wasn't aware that others knew Its location. There was, most likely, another reason she didn't look at the craft on her roof. What if she looked, and It wasn't there?

She was alone in the room with a corpse wet with her juices. It was still. She listened to the wind. The only movement was her breathing. Margaret stood like that until Adrian came. Until Adrian spoke at the other end of the apartment, Margaret hadn't really looked at what used to be Owen.

As Adrian walked in, Owen was lying face down on her bed with his pants off, and her girlfriend was standing in the doorway staring out into space. "What the fuck is going on in here?" accused Adrian. What the hell is she doing? Adrian seethed. Checking out the weather? She should be begging my forgiveness at this point, thought Adrian angrily, but she doesn't even look embarrassed. Then Margaret turned and stared at her blankly. Adrian caught herself thinking, Margaret looks beautiful, beautiful and innocent, like a little kid. But she didn't want Margaret to see. Because Adrian found herself seized with jealousy. As she stared at Margaret's white face, the blonde wandered over and with surprising calm announced, "He's dead."

Sarcastically Adrian replies, "Really?" This cunt is too much, she thinks, as she moves beside Owen. In her most loud and authoritative voice, Adrian wakes him. "Hey! What's wrong with you, get up!" But Owen doesn't move, he doesn't respond. Oh shit, thinks Adrian as she cups her hand under his nose to feel for his breath. Holy shit! This man is cold as a stone.

Margaret was glad that Adrian was there. Adrian will know what to do, she told herself. Adrian knows everything. As her romantic elation dissipated, an impassive acceptance of whatever Adrian dictated took its place.

"Did you kill him?" asked Adrian with an excited admiration. Although she knew it could bring unprecedented troubles, if Margaret had really done it, punished him for his lechery, Adrian would be proud.

"No," said Margaret, frightened. You lie, said the voice in her head. It's your own fault. You caused it. As if to confirm her own accusations, Adrian's voice echoed, "But you've been fucking him, right?"

Margaret was frozen with fear. But she was helpless when
it came to Adrian. She was in her hands, subject to her
whim. Margaret couldn't lie to Adrian. Not to her. She
knew it was her fault. She had done a terrible thing. Her
fright made her neck stiff. After what seemed like an eter-
nity, she managed to respond. Margaret's head bobbed up
and down in acquiescence.

"He's old, so he died here," said Adrian dramatically. "I
told you not to fuck with him. So now, he's dead." That's
what you get when you don't listen to me, my darling,
thought Adrian triumphantly. Without Owen to question
everything we do, life will be better, thought Adrian,
pleased. "Shit!" she exclaimed, realizing their predicament. "What are we gonna do now? If the cops come for
him and find the stuff, we'll both be in prison for a long
time, baby." A paranoiac panic seized Adrian. "You don't
understand," she spit at the impassive blonde. "The cops
have been after me for a long time." They're just waiting
for a chance to get in here, she worried. "They won't blame
it on you, they're gonna blame it on me," she said, gripping
Margaret's arm. They'll say I did it to get me off the street,
she thought to herself, just another pusher effectively in-
carcerated. The familiar image of barred windows pressed
through Adrian's mind. "They wanna nail me to the cross,"
she squawked, letting her panic show. A seldom seen fur-
row creased her brow. "Everybody's after me, the cops, the
junkies," said Adrian hysterically, "even you."

Margaret readily caught Adrian's panic. She had been
relying on Adrian's renowned ability to handle any situation. But Adrian couldn't take charge of it. It was overwhelming even for her. No! She doesn't want to handle it,
thought Margaret in a motionless frenzy. 'Cause Adrian
blames me. She thinks it is my fault. She will never help me.
She hates me for getting her involved, Margaret thought,

feeling attacked. Margaret couldn't speak, she was so frightened. She began to shake uncontrollably.

"They're gonna kill me," Adrian chanted wildly. "Jesus, help me. Jesus, help me. Jesus, help me," she whispered as she swayed, her eyes clenched tight. Suddenly, she stopped moving, opened her eyes, and looked at the trembling Margaret. I'll take some speed and straighten all this mess out, decided Adrian firmly. I always think clear on speed, if I take the right dosage; then I'll know what to do. Confidently she reached out to Margaret and rubbed her shaking shoulders. I have to take care of her, she thought righteously. I always took care of everybody; I'll figure out what to do. "Never mind," Adrian ordered Margaret. "I've had worse things happen to me." She took a vial of pills out of her skirt and spilled the contents in her miniature palm. Selecting two blue ones she pinched off from the others, Adrian said, "You calm down," and deposited them in Margaret's mouth. Then she took one large black pill for herself, swallowed it, and announced, "I'll take another speed and concentrate on this problem. You calm down."

Margaret felt around on the floor surrounding the bed, and found her discarded flask. She used a few drops of the residue to help the pills lodged in her throat on their merry way, making sure to leave as much liquid as possible for Adrian. Then she handed the flask to her girlfriend, grateful for her authority. The familiar ritual was calming to Margaret, even if the idea of Adrian on speed was not. They sat on the bed next to Owen, zombies on the life raft, waiting for the pills to work. When Adrian started to sweat, Margaret knew she was getting off. Margaret watched Adrian working herself into a kind of trance, swaying to some inner thoughts with her eyes clenched. She tried not to worry about their situation, to do what Adrian said. But she didn't find the display in her line of vision very reassuring: Adrian, practicing her hocus-pocus, swaying like some creature from the loony bin, right next to Owen's naked ass.

Magically, it seemed to Margaret, Adrian looked up, as though she had never been in a trance, and announced with bright eyes and a clear voice, "We should give him his last rites." That's the solution to all this? thought Margaret, perplexed. "What do you mean?" she answered cautiously, a foreboding wave of distrust crossing her entrails. "I'm a Catholic, baby," Adrian answered satanically. "A guy shouldn't go to hell without his last rites." "What are you gonna do?" demanded Margaret, openly suspicious. "You'll see," said a pleased Adrian, jumping off the bed. "Help me," she demanded, pulling a corner of the mirror plastic off the floor.

Margaret did all Adrian said automatically. Her mind was elsewhere. Sylvia and Johann had a date with destiny, after all, and they couldn't be kept waiting. In future, when she would survey the scene in her apartment, Margaret would be surprised at what Adrian had created there, even though she had helped to accomplish it. People always said Margaret was "spaced out"; she heard it all her life. It had become so natural for her to hear it that she came to believe it was expected of her. Eventually, she literally did occupy another space and time, so she couldn't recognize what her own hands had done. Her story was engrossing, so much more gratifying than her life.

Sylvia stared at the stoic stranger and tried to not appear as uncomfortable as she felt. She didn't want to give up her dream of a delectable date. Although he had been talking about his "research" in the most discreet of terms, as far as she could discern, this stranger wanted to watch some heroin dealers from her window. "So, you're looking for heroin and you don't want the police to know about it?

Hmmm?" Sylvia said as lightly as possible. What have you gotten yourself into, she chastised herself.

"What can I do?" said Johann enthusiastically, happy to share his frustration. "Nobody really knows the true nature of these aliens." Finally he had met someone intelligent and understanding with whom to share the complexity of his predicament. Very few people are special enough to have kind of imagination my situation requires. How lucky I am, he thought as he explained, to have found this remarkable person. "We must understand what the aliens find attractive about this underground lifestyle. The American scientists don't want to support our research officially . . ."

"You are from Germany," Sylvia interrupted knowingly. Perhaps history plays a part in their decision not to fund this project, she thought righteously.

"Yes, from Berlin," Johann replied enthusiastically. The whole world knows how we pride ourselves on the efficiency with which we complete our tasks, he thought proudly.

Let's see what turns this lumbering giant over, thought Sylvia. "I am Jewish," she replied provocatively. I don't mind kinky, I don't even mind bondage, I don't mind anything, as long as it's sex, thought the producer. Sylvia gave him a moment to chew on that, and then continued her inquiry with her most charming delivery. "So, what kind of connection can there be between UFOs and heroin?"

Johann Hoffmann did not understand the woman's comment in its context, but he thought he could understand Sylvia's face and vocal inflection. If I'm not mistaken, he thought to himself anxiously, this remark was some attempt at sexual provocation. But what does that have to do with race? he puzzled. I will try and sound more American, he decided. Then maybe it will be more understandable to

both of us "what's happening." "That's the point," Johann
said, imitating the American scientist he had met at the lab
in Berlin. "We already got a bunch of cases like that. The
saucers always land in a shooting gallery where there's a lot
of smack. It was happening in Germany, Japan, England;
and now it's happening here."

Sylvia tried not to let her disbelief show. An open mind is
what I need now, she told herself. It would be too cruel, too
sad a joke if I have planned the evening with the purpose of
seducing a mentally ill giant. "You have seen a UFO?" she
inquired as lightly as possible, trying not to let her fear
show. He doesn't even sound like a scientist, she thought to
herself, discouraged.

"This morning!" Johann said with a broad smile. "That's
why I'm here."

"Oh. That's very interesting," Sylvia said with a dead
face. "Would you like a drink?" Because I need one, she
thought, perplexed.

Johann smiled excitedly at her. "You can see it as well!"
he said brightly, his voice booming.

"You are telling me I can see a UFO?" Sylvia said with a
deadpan delivery. She thought, I really need a drink.

"Yes, through your window," he replied.

"How fascinating," she said hopefully. "You mean I can
walk over there and look through the window and see a
UFO?" He wouldn't lie so obviously, she thought, her spir-
its climbing as she prayed that he was a well man.

"No," said Johann manipulatively. "But you can see it
through my telescope," he suggested in calmly measured
tones. Oh shit, thought Sylvia, this man is a loony.

"You carry a telescope with you?" she demanded caustically. Of course it would be too easy, too nice if I could have
verified his sanity by simply looking out the window, she
thought, depressed.

"In this case," Johann said happily, referring to his strange black valise. How clever I am, he thought. Now she will want me to set it up to satisfy her own curiosity.

"How nice," Sylvia said sarcastically. "Why don't you set it up?" she challenged. "I have always dreamed about seeing a UFO." I'm getting too old for these emotional roller-coaster rides, she thought wearily. I get enough of this shit at the office. "What was it you said you were drinking?" she queried, as she relished the thought of a stiff drink releasing her knotted neck.

He tried to control the impulsive grin from spreading across his face. For a moment he was a kid whose mommy had given him permission to set up his erector set. She was gonna let him do it! Johann tried to force the corners of his mouth down. He struggled with his facial features while his mind exploded with glee. All that tedious arranging had come to something; he was going to get to continue his research.

As Sylvia strode to the kitchen, she tried not to notice how goofy the scientist looked as he struggled with his emotions. Where did I get the idea this man was elegant? she asked herself, cringing. Sylvia kicked off her shoes and enjoyed the cool tile on her blood-filled feet. Methodically, she took the ice cubes from the refrigerator, dumped them from the plastic tray, and listened for the unique clatter of ice against glass as she guided them into the crystal pitcher. The sound evoked relief and a voracious watering in her mouth. Sylvia postponed the process of fixing her drink, absorbing all the sensual details. The soft light at the end of the day, the silence save for the clattering ice, the feel of her crystal, the look of her fine glass. She luxuriated in the moments up to the first sip. She loved her little ritual. It obliterated all else.

It was Adrian's resonate voice vibrating in Margaret's

lungs that brought her back to the room. For a moment, Margaret didn't know where she was. Adrian chanted as she pounded her miniature fist into her other open hand. The man was wrapped in foil like a Popsicle, or a bouquet of flowers, his head being the blossom. He was lying on her bed with his eyes closed, and the small girl was singing, or rather, reciting a poem over his head. There were candles everywhere, which flickered unevenly and caused eerie patterns of orange to cross over the trio's faces. But then the sun going down cast a dull orange glow over everyone, without the aid of the candle flame. As Margaret recognized the foil as being the reflector plastic that had been left behind by a fashion photographer, the events of the recent past rushed into her brain. Owen is dead, she realized. She looked at the sweating Adrian in shock. Instantly the words of the chant became recognizable.

> "So you're dead now, shit.
> And you're going to hell.
> Straight from your marijuana jungles.
> Straight from your lies, your lies, your lies.
> You dropped dead fucking.
> It suits you well.
> You go to hell."

Margaret listened in horror to the too-true words being uttered. Do I really belong with this monster? she thought, as the cruel words fell on her heart. Do I belong to this? This group of gremlins? More than to the dream world of the sixties, a voice in her head answered.

Margaret remembered evenings of weed and art films: stoned men patronizing the opinions of women, and herself, Margaret, the sex kitten. Too stoned to even understand the film, frightened that the other women might find out and disclaim her, but a favorite with the guys. So pretty, so young, so eager to please, a tool to fight off the newly competitive female peers who had become scary to Owen and his cronies. It had never occurred to Margaret that her lack of understanding, her inability to defend herself or form an opinion might have to do with her drug intake. Back then, she didn't know she couldn't handle potent pot. Margaret assumed she was stupid like everyone else. They had always treated her like she was; she had had no reason to believe that she wasn't.

Owen really believed that they changed the world. What's changed? thought Margaret. The rich run everything and have all the power. Women are dependent on their husbands for whatever they can bring home to put on the table. Love is a dependence trap which reduces the female to the level of a child. For all their proselytizing about equal rights for women and blacks and poor people, nothing came of it, because they didn't address the seat of the power, which is the economic base. The only evidence I can see of change is that it's that a lot easier to kill yourself, thought Margaret. Drugs are more plentiful and more socially acceptable, thanks to all those "freedom fighters."

> "You spent your life doing three things:
> Fucking, smoking pot, and lying.
> Shit.
> You thought you found the righteous way.
> But you deceived them all and now you'll pay.
> You go to hell, it suits you well.
> Shit."

Margaret stared at her living lover. The perspiration was beading on her demure upper lip as Adrian's fist pounded her own thigh to get the perfect thumping sound. Adrian is in her glory, thought Margaret, a little shocked by her realization. This miniature woman revels in any kind of drama, and will do anything to push a situation to the edge. Living on the edge; is that what I'm doing? Margaret thought to herself. She was watching Adrian conduct a horrible ritual for the death of her Owen. This is what my life has come to, she observed coolly.

> "We'll all go to hell.
> I'll go to hell too.
> But I know I'm damned,
> And you never knew.
> You thought you found the righteous way.
> But you deceived yourself,
> And now you'll pay.
> Marijuana jungles float away."

Marijuana jungles float away, thought Margaret. Float away with my Owen. Poor sweet Owen, reflected Margaret. Now he's dead and it's my fault. Maybe he's better off, considered the bleached blonde. Maybe it's a relief to be dead. At least if I was with him I wouldn't be alone. He was lucky, he knew where he belonged. But where's my generation, where's my people? Now he's dead and I'm left alone with Adrian. I'm left alone with a drug dealer, the death dealer Adrian. If I told her that that's what I called her, she'd probably like it, mused Margaret. I'm so tired, she thought, what I need is a rest.

> "You dreamt about love,
> While you smoked your pot.
> You thought it was real.
> I knew it was not.
> We live in hell.
> I know it well.
> I am aware.
> And I love my own nightmare.

Shit.
So you weren't ready for the toll of the bell.
And for me it's easy from hell to hell.
I'm not dancing in marijuana jungles.
I live in concrete mazes,
Stone and glass.
Hard like my heart.
Sharp and clean,
With no romantic illusions
Of changing the world.
I don't lie to myself
that love can cure.
Because I know I'm alone.
You fought that every day you lived.
You lied, you lied, you lied.
You go to hell.
It suits you well.
Shit."

Margaret looked at Adrian, her face drooping with grief and fatigue. She stared at Owen, as the candle wax dripped on his still flesh. "So now it's time," Margaret said softly. "I'll try your heroin."

Adrian smiled slyly. She couldn't believe her luck. Owen dead and now she would have Margaret under total control. Finally Margaret wouldn't dare to criticize her with her vicious mouth. She will be too scared that I might cut off her supply, thought Adrian triumphantly. "That's good. Good girl," Adrian carefully cooed. She didn't want to do anything that would scare Margaret off her new decision.

"I'll shoot it up and then I'll die," Margaret stated undramatically.

"Are you crazy?" answers Adrian, astonished. Sometimes she sounds just like my mom, thinks Adrian, full of bullshit. She's just trying to jerk me around.

"I'll kill myself as they all did. I wanna die," says Margaret provocatively. So many of this crazy crook's friends are overdosing, and still she pretends she's immune to the malady. Even though she's providing the means, thinks Margaret angrily. So what if she only snorts? One day when she's older, she'll get depressed, weaken, and start to shoot. She claims to live in the "real" world, but she wouldn't know the truth if it were staring her in the face.

"Don't say that!" Adrian commands threateningly. It's not true! Margaret can't say that! thinks Adrian, as she panics. "They didn't kill themselves. They are being killed by this bourgeois society. I am not going to die! They will not kill me! They killed Janis Joplin and Jimmy Hendrix and Sid Vicious. And they killed Peter, and Patricia, and Mike. They create this legend that all of us should die young. Well, I am not going to die. I'm going to live to be a hundred."

Margaret smiled a superior smile and said lightly, "So don't die." That, at least, is my choice, Margaret soothed herself. "Everybody has a personal choice, whether to live or to die." She sighed knowingly.

"Are your brains fried?" demanded Adrian loudly. How can she be so passive?! Passive like Mom, she thought nervously. But I'm not like her. I'm nothing like my mom.

"Nobody wants to die," answered Adrian, superior. Margaret's just a stupid cunt, what does she know? thought Adrian. She's crazy and stupid. It's a good thing she's so dumb or it might be dangerous for me to be around her; with that mental illness in my blood and all.

"People throw gasoline on themselves and set themselves on fire," Margaret said calmly.

Adrian remembered Margaret showing her pictures of

draft dodgers burning. At the time, she hadn't understood her point. "Political fanatics," spit Adrian.

"Nine hundred fourteen in Guyana," Margaret said knowingly.

"Religious fanatics," answered Adrian, thinking, Margaret is just trying to trick me. She wasn't going to let the images of the mass suicide in Jonestown haunt her.

"And what kind of fanatics are your clients?" asked Margaret ominously.

It was just what Margaret's drug involvement was supposed to prevent. Once she gets going she can't keep her trap shut, thought a panicked Adrian. Always talkin' too fast; too fast for me to think. I'll fix her. I'll shut her up, Adrian swore furiously.

Swiftly Adrian scooped the joint from the pot bowl near the window. Instantly it was in dead Owen's mouth with a match pressed to it. "Do you smoke marijuana in hell, fucker?" shouted Adrian triumphantly. She pushed on his chest. Miraculously, the smoke billowed up around them. Margaret was consumed with fright, reminded of earlier fears that Adrian was involved with evil powers. How could anyone so bad not be? "He's smoking!" said Adrian, delighted. "Help me do it, Margaret!"

Sylvia's toes opened out onto the carpet as she walked across her living room to the window. How good it felt to be relaxing with a drink in hand, barefoot in her lovely home, a gentleman caller at her window. Carefully she made her way to him, mindful not to spill the two drinks she ferried on her brand-new plush-pile, wall-to-wall carpet. She watched the fluid lap at the lip of the glasses, certain that just as her eyes were on the alcohol, his eyes were on her. She was sorely disappointed when she reached her destination. Johann Hoffmann wasn't even aware of her presence. "So . . ." she queried as he peered through his shiny and impressive telescope, "can you see this flying saucer?"

Johann Hoffmann had been completely absorbed in watching the activities of the lowlife beings across the canyon of buildings. He had never seen behavior of this kind before; it had him entranced. He didn't know what to say to the formidable woman standing behind him holding dripping goblets. "Ahhh . . . ugh. Wait a minute," he said, baffled. "OK. I am waiting," Sylvia replied charmingly.

Margaret was in a state of shock. She felt frozen. Her thoughts weighed her down to the point of inaction. She watched helplessly as Adrian, monkeylike, pressed on Owen's dead body. The joint burned bright with Owen's lungs as bellows. Finally Margaret managed to utter, "Don't do it!" her entire being crying out in frustration, How did I get here? What am I doing here? The scene before her had so little to do with her picture of herself in the world.

"You don't like it, baby?" said Adrian, pleased. "I always dreamed to fuck a dead man, now's my chance."

"You're crazy," muttered Margaret softly.

"Sure I am, baby. That's why you like me," Adrian replies gleefully. As if involved in an erotic conspiracy Adrian suggests, "So let's fuck him."

"Don't you touch him," Margaret warns threateningly.

"If you don't like it, baby," Adrian deliberately provokes, "you don't have to watch."

Slowly Adrian pulls the edge of her skirt up revealing the flesh of her thighs. Walking on her knees, she creeps close to the body, then straddles Owen's peaceful face. Laying the circle skirt dramatically full around her, Adrian smiles and closes her eyes. Subtly she slips her pelvis front to back.

Margaret watched, her mouth agape. Adrian was really fucking the face of her dead Owen. She was stunned.

Freaks, she thought, A couple of freaks. A circus of uncontrolled sick people. That's what they would say. That's what they would know, if anyone saw us.

So this is what kind of behavior interests the alien, thought the scientist, fascinated, as he peered through his telescope. Although it could be that it's just a side effect of a drug-oriented life, Johann altercated. To make an accurate determination I should study in depth the behavior patterns of these drug takers. I should take notes, and document their various activities. But the woman will not understand, he realizes, suddenly aware that Sylvia was still holding the heavy, dripping vials. "I'm afraid you shouldn't see what I see," he confessed to her soberly.

"That's funny," Sylvia replied threateningly. "You can see it and I cannot. You are a private detective," she accused knowingly. "I thought this was for science."

"Yes," said Johann, thinking grandly, For science . . . Women, are delicate creatures, he ruminated. He could see through the corner of his eagle eye, by glancing through the lens, that the gyrations of the small one were getting stronger. Then his mind reeled at thought of a woman witnessing such vile antics. His background and conditioning would not allow it. "But you really shouldn't see this," he informed her.

"What are you afraid of?" Sylvia demanded boldly.

It should be over in a moment, thought Johann, judging from his own sexual experience. "Wait a minute," he countered.

"What's going on?" Sylvia demanded shrilly, her hands tired from holding the wet glasses. "I can't see it. I shouldn't see it. Can the police see it?" she said angrily.

She will ruin everything if she tells, Johann thought, distressed. Silly woman! She doesn't understand what this is about. "This alien is killing people," he insisted, as calmly as he could muster.

"Let the police deal with the killing of people," Sylvia countered, enjoying her power.

Carefully Johann answered. He wanted to sound more American, but he found the wording too simple. He was worried that he might sound too patronizing. Johann didn't want to make her angry. "If the police are involved, they will not be able to handle it. More people will be killed. It happened before."

As the shock wore off, rage filled Margaret's numb body. I will not allow it, her mind screamed, as a shout, "Nooooo!" escaped her lips. She propelled her body at Adrian's slight frame, knocking her off Owen's face. Instantly agile Adrian rolled to her feet. She found Margaret arranged off the edge of the bed, avoiding conflict, as her purpose had been fulfilled. "Why did you have to do that?" Margaret asked earnestly. "Why?"

"Don't get moral with me, whore," snarled Adrian. "You had to fuck him, right?" she demanded, outraged. "Didn't I tell you not to fuck him? Didn't I?"

I can't allow this warped girl to dictate to me, thought Margaret. Everything is too crazy. If I do, that means I've really lost control. It's the only freedom I have left, doing what I want with who I want. She's too sick to know what's wrong or right. It's my life, Margaret asked herself, isn't it? "This is my place. I'll do what I want here," she stated defiantly. She may pay the rent, thought Margaret, concerned, but the lease is still in my name. It's a good thing she has a cash business and never pays by check.

"You mean you can fuck any petty asshole who gives you a chance," she retaliated. "You're a god damn whore!" Adrian accused with wonder and disgust.

Margaret slung her long arm across the space between

them. Her hand stung as it made contact with Adrian's baby face. Her mind screamed denial, but Vincent's attack was still fresh in her brain. More than that, her desire to please Owen but not herself. She cannot call me that! a voice screamed in her head. It was the worst thing to be where she came from. The town she had grown up in was still largely puritan. "Don't *you* call *me* that, you low-class freaky monster! Monster!" screeched Margaret.

People had called Adrian monster before. The wound reopened and hatred flowed forth. She jumped forward and latched onto the small shock of hair still left on Margaret's bleached head. Pulling hard, she shouted, "I'm a monster? They all fuck you. You let these guys walk on your bones, bitch. You're gonna kill me with syphilis one day, you dirty cunt!"

"Don't talk to me like that," Margaret retorted with rage. "Your mother was nuts and your father was a bum. You'll never go anywhere but to the Bowery. You belong with the bums." Margaret stood, pulling Adrian with her. As she grabbed her small frame and Adrian released the hold on her hair, Adrian fell on Owen's body with a resounding thud. For a moment Margaret was paralyzed with the horror of it.

Adrian was stunned that Margaret had gathered enough information about her background to understand where she came from. But no one could ever mention her family in such a way. Pride was all her poor Italian papa had passed on to her. She was forced to retaliate. Adrian Bianchi could not condone an attack on her sweet, sad dad. She knew what to do. She had done it before. She pulled the knife with deliberate skill and flicked open the slender switchblade, flashing it before Margaret's painted eyes. "Now what did you say?" she demanded confidently, brandishing the blade dangerously close to the white, freckled skin of Margaret's angular face. Unless Margaret takes it back, I will cut her—scar her for life for insulting my family, decides Adrian zealously.

I am not going to let her use these reform-school tactics on me, thinks the long-legged Yankee. I am not a child and I refuse to be involved in this juvenile violence. With controlled rage Margaret answers, "You heard me."

"Take it back," screams Adrian, brandishing the knife between them. "Take it back!"

"Get out of my place, you low-class freak," answers Margaret regally, disgusted by her participation in the childish quarrel.

"Watch your mouth or I'll cut your face. Then nobody will fuck your ugly cunt!" enraged Adrian growls. The knife pokes forward, just missing Margaret's belly as she jumps back, hollowing her torso. "I'll fix you," bellows Adrian.

The prospect of getting sliced filled Margaret with nausea, but her rage was stronger than her fear. She knew that size was on her side, and grabbing the agile Adrian's elbow, she tried to wiggle the knife from her grasp. But years of experience reigned on the singer's side. Not only did she hold onto the knife, but soon the blade came dangerously close to Margaret's ear. As she released Adrian's arm for her ear's sake, Margaret jumped aside just as Adrian lunged. Margaret was then able to grab her girlfriend's wrist, but her painted cork platform shoes had become tangled in the stretched Orlon that covered the bed. The women toppled over, four hands still clutching the knife. As they lay front to front, Margaret angrily pushed her knee into Adrian's abdomen. Adrian was caught off guard and lost her balance, allowing Margaret to throw her weight over Adrian's frame. Digging her fingers into Adrian's grasp, Margaret was able to free one arm. But this arm soon wrapped around Margaret's head, blinding her for the brief moment it took for Adrian to grasp her hair. As Adrian pulled Margaret's head back by her hair, Margaret whacked Adrian's arm against the edge of the bed, freeing the knife. As the knife fell to the floor, pain shot down Adrian's arm, but she deftly rolled to her feet, ignoring her discomfort. As her soles hit the floor, she turned quickly, only to see Margaret scoop up the weapon. Adrian was on her in a flash; she jumped onto her back and threw Margaret on the bed. Together they rolled over Owen's carcass, struggling to gain control over the weapon. When Margaret glanced sideways and saw she was on the corpse, her resolve weakened. Suddenly Adrian was on top of her. Margaret, with her long arms, held the knife just out of Adrian's grasp, her head wedged between Owen's and Adrian's. Margaret stared at her dead Owen. Her outrage at Adrian's disrespect gave Margaret a newfound strength. She rallied her energy and miraculously rose from the bed, carrying Adrian to her feet as well, in an unbelievable rush of fury. It was Margaret now striking out with the weapon in an uncontrolled frenzy. But surprise didn't dampen Adrian's instincts. Dodging Margaret's impulsive jabs, Adrian threw a kick. Her foot sailed with certainty into Margaret's belly, throwing her against the wall, and causing the knife to sail across the room. Adrian scrambled after it. It took her a while to find it, as she had not seen where it landed. She was only mildly curious why Margaret had not scrambled after her; she had, after all, witnessed where it landed. Adrian turned, brandishing the knife, ready for action, only to see a docile young woman kneeling under and hanging on a full-length white dress. If her thumb had been in her mouth, it would have made the picture a complete replay of her brother hanging onto his security blanket as it dried on the clothesline on the roof of their old apartment building. Adrian quickly moved to stand over her, but Margaret didn't seem to react to her presence. She remained docile even as Adrian pressed the knife to her throat. "He was a good man," Margaret whispered in a daze. "He never did anything to you."

It was her passivity that stopped Adrian from slitting Margaret's throat. She knew it wouldn't be satisfying 'cause Margaret didn't seem to care. "You're not worth the trouble," Adrian said smugly, trying to hide that her victory didn't feel satisfying. Then suddenly Adrian felt unusually calm, a rare state for her. She wouldn't know it was the relaxation that comes from expending so much physical energy. Adrian had never exercised.

When they were finally quiet, Johann quickly allowed his hostess to peer through his instrument. "You want to see the alien craft?" Johann asked generously. "Look . . ." he said taking the drinks from Sylvia's grasp, "you will see it." He hoped the humans would not start to get active during the short time she would be watching, and he adjusted the telescope to include only the image of the spaceship. But Johann noticed that as she put her hand on the shaft of the telescope, Sylvia inadvertently readjusted its position.

Sylvia took in the vision of the brightly decorated apartment, the oddly dressed girls, and the still gentleman; then she announced with surprise, "That's a dead body!"

Swiftly Johann pushed on the barrel of the telescope, and authoritatively suggested, "Now let me see." Automatically Sylvia moved aside, allowing him to look through the lens. Swiftly he readjusted his telescope, setting its sight on his pride and joy. He hoped the new subject would distract her and take her mind off the earlier, surly sight. Proudly Johann spurted, "That's an alien craft."

It took Sylvia a moment to identify the disc next to the plastic Coke bottle as the object of interest Johann was so excited about. "That's the UFO?" she queried impulsively. "Isn't it kind of small?"

"The alien craft is about the size of a dinner plate," Johann informed her calmly. "Who ever told you that aliens need as much space as people?" the scientist joked with the little woman.

Sylvia was taken aback for a moment. If her new friend was indeed a lunatic, then an adjustment in his sense of reality could make him berserk. However, where could he have gotten such a sophisticated piece of equipment if he wasn't a scientist? Perhaps he is a crazy scientist? she asked herself. "Isn't it possible," she queried delicately, "that that object may be a child's toy, and not a UFO?"

Johann thought angrily, When they all die then you'll believe me. "Just watch a little longer," he said calmly, leaning over the machine to check its instruments. "You will see for yourself what will happen there." He was adept at masking his emotions, and from earlier encounters at the institute knew not to let his anger show.

As his jacket brushed her shoulder Sylvia swooned and sighed to herself. Finally, she thought, I thought this joker would never make his move. She tilted her head back, to make it easier for him to get to her lips, and said in her deepest low voice, sucking in his odor, "That's a nice world you show me, where scientists are as big as the Empire State Building; and aliens are as big as . . . jumbo shrimp." It was a lot to say well in one breath, and even more difficult since her mouth was watering.

Even as inexperienced as Johann was, he knew that it was a strange thing to say. He didn't know what jumbo shrimp had to do with anything. Still, he smiled, thinking, That must be a compliment. Suddenly he was aware of the unusual amount of heat rising from her body; and noticed that she had changed her apparel. He wondered when she had taken the time out to change out of her business suit, and into the Japanese gown. He answered her uncertainly, unaccustomed to the confusing rush of emotion. "I have available no other world to show you," he said quietly.

Adrian was concerned by Margaret's unblinking gaze. She was often absorbed in some daydream, but this time it was more than usual. Adrian was creeped out by her stony stare. She pushed her snout into Margaret's face and said soothingly, "Don't worry. Calm down, baby. Calm down. Everything will be all right. We'll leave this fucking place; go to Berlin. I'll sing in the nightclubs. Germans love me. We'll be happy."

Apparently these two girls are lovers, Sylvia said to herself as she watched the small one comfort the tall one. At least someone is getting loved around here, she thought bitterly. "Are you sure this has something to do with a UFO?" she queried, as she noticed her guest hadn't touched his drink. "It looks like two women just killed a man."

"Just watch," the scientist assured her. "This is not my first encounter with the alien."

Adrian had thought that Margaret had not heard what she said. Suddenly Margaret turned her head and stared eerily at her from her engrossing stupor. "What are we gonna do with his body?" Margaret demanded.

Adrian was energized. Action was what she was good at. "Don't worry, I know what to do," she bragged. "You want to do it right now?" she asked her leggy roommate, relieved to finally have an audience. "OK," Adrian answered herself, not wanting to lose Margaret's attention. "But you have to help me," she playfully warned her. Adrian knew that it was best to keep Margaret active. After all, she reasoned, the girl ain't right in her head, and that's the remedy for almost everything, even an OD.

Margaret languidly pulled each piece of clothing from the long box, as Adrian had directed her to empty it. She tried to remember where the swatches of cloth came from. Each one looked familiar, but she couldn't remember if she had ever worn them. Where did this come from? she agonized over each piece. Even Adrian's growl, "Hurry up," didn't stop her painful querying.

It's taking an awfully long time for her to empty that box, Adrian worried.

"Why don't they call the police," wondered the ever practical Sylvia as she watched the women move around the room.

"They don't want the police to be involved," Johann answered nervously.

"Why?" Sylvia insisted.

"You know, everyone has their reasons for not wanting the authorities in their home," Johann said suggestively. He was hoping that Sylvia had stashed a bit of marijuana . . . anything; any little thing to discourage her from wanting to deal with the police. With the thought of police, Johann's mouth watered for a taste of the alcoholic beverage. The police reminded him of the times he had woken up in jail after a *sauftour*. I'm controlling myself very well, he thought. For Science . . . he told himself proudly as he gazed at the still full cocktail glass. *"They* have a very good reason," he continued. "They have heroin there."

Sylvia watched as the girls pulled the lifeless remains into the large cardboard coffin they had pulled from the closet. After sealing it, the strange creatures carried it, one at either end, out the roof door, and far from the apartment interior. The disparity in their heights made the task difficult without handles. The tall one struggled to move the unappealing burden in her high, uncomfortable shoes. In her short skirt, high shoes, and strange hairdo, she looked like an exotic bird to Sylvia. A couple of times, Sylvia thought they were going to drop their burden. Too bad they don't have a man around the house to help them carry things, thought Sylvia sympathetically. In this weather, she worried, it won't be long before this dead man starts to smell. She looked at the large male beside her, and was glad not to be alone with her thoughts after seeing the corpse. "I sure wouldn't like to be in their shoes right now," Sylvia said gratefully as she looked into Johann's big eyes.

Johann laughed, amused by Sylvia's little joke. Funny to think of either of them in *that* situation, he thought. We would never be involved with drugs. "No," he said, pleased with the woman, "I wouldn't like it either."

Margaret had been doing what she was told automatically. But as Adrian sat on the box to rest, Margaret came out of her daydream, to look at her wicked girlfriend resting, unperturbed, her ass over dead Owen's head. Adrian patted the box beside her, indicating that Margaret should join her on the cardboard coffin. Margaret did as she was told, despite the ominous feeling that they were doing something immoral by sitting on the dead man. She waited for the next set of instructions, wanting to believe that Adrian knew what she was doing. When none were forthcoming, Margaret demanded, "What do we do now?"

What an idiot, thought Adrian. It's obvious. "We'll just leave him here," she said impatiently. "We're going to Berlin."

"Sure," said Margaret sarcastically. That's what I get for trusting a criminal to help me in a crisis, she thought angrily.

We need some kind of ceremony to satisfy this puritan's sense of duty, Adrian cleverly calculated. "We should have a wake," she said enthusiastically, as though she was agreeing with her friend.

We're not prepared to entertain anyone, thought Margaret, perplexed. You can't give a funeral party improperly. "There's no food," she informed her ill-bred friend. There's never any food in this house, she thought, missing her full refrigerator, like when she lived with Owen.

"So what's the problem?" wondered Adrian. Boy, is this girl hard to please today, she thought. "I'll bring it, baby," she said lovingly. "I'll go to the store and get some food."

When I was with Owen, he always went to the store for me, remembered Margaret. He was sweet to me and I was bored. There were no bodies then, no drugs, just life as usual. The refrigerator was always full. Now it seems like a joke when my lover goes grocery shopping. "Owen liked chicken," Margaret said earnestly. "He knew all the different ways to make chicken: chicken roasted, chicken boiled, chicken baked with apples. He would go to the store and buy me chicken. Lots of them. He always bought me birds."

Finally, a ritual that will make this bitch happy, thought Adrian. "You want to fix a chicken, baby?" she asked patronizingly. "A chicken for Owen?"

"Yes," said Margaret, trying to hurt her present lover. "A big chicken."

"OK," said Adrian agreeably. "If you want to play house, I don't mind. We'll make a celebration, and right afterward, we'll leave this fucking place. We'll just disappear," Adrian said, excited. "We won't tell anybody that we're going to Berlin."

For the longest time the scientist didn't move. He just stared through the lens. Sylvia was bored to tears. But she knew that flattery would get her everywhere. She was, after all, a producer. "Your research is very dangerous," Sylvia said seductively.

It was a moral question that kept running through the scientist's mind. He knew that fairly soon deaths would

occur there. How could he, as a man of science, allow that
to happen without acting? He had, by way of watching,
gotten rather attached to the funny characters across the
concrete canyon. "They are in danger, not me," he per-
functorily answered the woman. They were after all, young
girls. Some one should warn them somehow, he decided.

Johann was paying no attention to her whatsoever. Sylvia
was pissed. "If it's so dangerous we should call the police,"
she said angrily.

"The police are no protection from aliens," the scientist
informed her. How many times do I have to tell her? he
thought, irritated.

"You are protection from aliens?" Sylvia demanded provocatively. "You carry a laser gun in your pants?" she said
sarcastically, looking at his crotch. Johann didn't react, he
was so surprised by her strange humor. When Sylvia didn't
get a response, she sighed, disappointed. "I think I need
another drink," she decided.

Margaret watched as Adrian gathered her belongings to
go out in the world. She's leaving me here, she noted,
wondering why that seemed so terrible. Margaret lay on the
bed, wondering what she would do with herself until
Adrian returned. I should get dressed for the wake, she
decided. I think I have just the thing, she assured herself,
remembering her sad purple-and-black-dyed garment.

A slightly soggy Sylvia returned from the kitchen to ob-
serve her observer. Her new glass was already only half full.
Johann noticed as she breathed on him. He didn't want to
be rude, so he interrupted his watching to smile at her. As
he did, the weaving woman plopped right into his large lap.
"You are brave, noble knight," Sylvia teased the scientist.
"Why don't you go and free these beauties from the
dragon?"

Rapidly, the Germanic giant rose, lifting Sylvia easily,

and deposited her in the still-warm seat. "That's exactly what I'm going to do," he announced, only half joking.

"You're not really going there?" said Sylvia angrily, sore at having been dumped out of his lap and informed that she was being abandoned.

"No," the scientist reassured her, flattered by her concern for his well-being. "The little one just went out, and I want to try and warn her."

"Are you serious?" fumed the furious producer.

"Yes," Johann replied, not really sure why she questioned his response. He watched as Sylvia straightened her garment, and stiffened in the chair.

"You really are brave," the woman stated regally. "You're the first man to ever leave me, right before we were about to have dinner."

"I'm sorry," Johann stuttered, as the woman's angry eyes burned into his. "I will be right back," he assured her. He wondered why she could not understand that the unusual circumstances forced him to be improper. As he put on his jacket, she continued to burden him with the blame.

"Well, don't expect me to wait for you," she said in a huff. "I have never eaten cold Chinese, and I don't intend to start liking it now."

"I'm very sorry," the German replied sincerely, suddenly frightened that she might not let him return. "But duty is more important than shrimp."

"The duty is yours, the house is mine," Sylvia stated curtly. "And in my house, shrimps are more important than duty."

Johann didn't know if she was joking or not. Just in case, he smiled, not wanting to offend his hostess, and hurried out of the suddenly smaller apartment.

Delusions and Princes

Margaret found solace in her occupation, creatively adorning her person. Her mind meandered pleasantly as she painted the pink and purple tears on the white face. Feeling quite pleased with her endeavor, she noted that the makeup went well with the full-length lace gown. Engrossed in the activity, she felt better than she had in a long time. Then that she realized she was not alone.

She caught his shadowy shape behind her in the makeup mirror. He stood in the darkened doorway watching her. She could only make out his silhouette. But Margaret soon figured out who it was. None of the people she knew had the easily recognizable paunch of middle age, except him. Of all the clients Adrian accommodated, he was the last one Margaret wanted to see. Why did Adrian leave the entrance unlocked, why? Margaret agonized. In case one of her customers needed to stop by for a fix, you jerk, she answered herself.

The fear Margaret experienced was overwhelming. But she didn't let it show. The one thought that stuck in her blank mind was not to let him sense her fear. If he could smell it, she knew, he would go after her like an animal. It had happened before. A frozen Margaret forced her hand to continue painting the purple tears. In measured strokes she continued her toilet. She did not want to let him know that she knew he was hiding there. She couldn't think anything, save the recurrent idea: Don't let him know that you're frightened. After what seemed like a long time, her mind wandered. She wondered, Why would he come here, when he could be at home with the perfect Katherine. Her preoccupation with his predicament gave Margaret a few moments of relief from the tension. And made Paul seem a little less frightening, a little more human.

She could imagine his disheveled shape sweating out the drug in Katherine's white eyelet comforter. Of course, it would be white, she thought, and either old-fashioned cotton and stretchy with dingle-balls, like my mother's, or stuffed with down.

Katherine looked smashing in her tight, tasteful, cocktail dress. "Paul?" she called softly to her leaking lover. "Darling, get up. Take a shower now. You're sweating all over the clean spread."

The voice came from far away. Before Paul identified it, the nausea carried him to consciousness. But he knew it wouldn't do any good to maneuver his cadaverous form into the bathroom. He would only get the dry heaves, and be more miserable than he already was. "I feel ill, Kathy," he said to his approaching angel, and slitted his orbs to view his benevolent beauty.

"I know you feel sick," Katherine sighed. "You've had drugs today."

"No, no, I didn't," Paul answered automatically. He didn't want to upset her with the truth. Paul had long ago decided she didn't want it.

"Get up, take a shower," Katherine suggested cheerfully. "You can't go to the party like that." She pulled the pillow playfully from under his head. "The guests are already starting to arrive," she whispered in mock morning. Everything was going smoothly and Katherine was looking forward to a successful evening.

The room spun as his head plopped on the sheet. He had forgotten about her damn party. She couldn't really expect him to participate. What he needed was tender, loving care. "Fuck the guests," he said angrily as he pulled her toward him.

Katherine resisted his tired tug, frozen in fright. In the past Paul had played his part well; he was a enjoyably humorous host. The success of Katherine's entertaining was due largely to Paul's irreverent sense of humor. "What do you mean, 'Fuck the guests'?" Katherine asked nervously. "Stop talking like that. Get up, take a shower," she urged.

"Fuck the guests. Fuck the shower," Paul reiterated loudly, as he sat up in the bed. The anger seemed to sap his energy. Immediately, Paul's frame uncoiled; as his head hit the pillow his mouth fell open. After a few raspy breaths, he drooled and slovenly stated, "I just want to lie here . . ."

Katherine was stunned. Already her clients had asked for Paul. She had disappeared from her own party to produce him. "Are you serious?" she pleaded softly, not wanting to believe the news.

"I am abso-fucking-lutely serious," Paul spit at her. She was trying to guilt him out, he knew. But this time it wasn't going to work. She was always good to him, too good. He didn't deserve her, that he knew. He often joked about it with her friends and clients. Well, I'm sick of it, he reasoned. Let them find another dog to kick. If there's one thing I can't stand, it's a martyr. Let her be a martyr for another man's sake. I can't do it anymore. It's too much pressure.

In all the time that they had been together, Paul had never sworn at her. He always swore at things, or other people, or about the situation, but never at her. It was one of the reasons she always told to herself for not giving up on him, that he always treated her like a lady. Now Katherine was at a loss. "You can't talk to me like that," she insisted.

"Why?" Paul said with a venom Katherine had never seen directed at her. "Why can't I?!" he repeated threateningly.

Katherine was hurt and confused. "Because . . ." she stuttered. "Because . . ."

"Because this is your place?" Paul roared. "Because you pay for everything?" he bellowed. Images of her happily sitting at her organized desk, sending off checks to companies haunted him. All the humiliations for all the restaurant tabs she ever paid came rushing back at him. He hated her. She always rubbed his nose in it, he decided.

"Paul, please let's not start on this subject now," Katherine pleaded.

"Why not?" he continued sadistically. "Why shouldn't we speak on this subject?" he demanded. "You started it, not me."

Suddenly Katherine's demeanor changed. She was, after all, entertaining her clients this evening. Her priorities became clear. "You want me to get upset," she stated regally. "You want me to cry and ruin my makeup and have an unpleasant evening. But I'm not going to cry. I'm going to go outside and receive my guests."

"You have your party," Paul pouted, interrupting her. Suddenly he felt very sorry for himself. "Leave me alone. I just want to sleep."

He can't sleep here, Katherine panicked. The guests have to pass through to get to the bathroom. How much can I afford to put up with? This time he's gone too far. Katherine's instincts took over. She was after all, a survivor. Angrily, she attacked him, saying all the things she was brought up never to say. "You ruined your career, so now you want to ruin mine," she stated knowingly. "You know I've invited everybody to this. You know how hard I've worked to make everything perfect. You haven't lifted a finger to help me. And now, you want to embarrass me in front of my clients. To show them you're a failure, that you take drugs, that you haven't made any money from your films, or books, or anything . . . But mostly you want to humiliate me, that's your point: that I'm such a fool for putting up with you. Well, if you don't like me, you should leave. This is my house. *Leave my house.* You either get dressed and behave like you have some self-respect, or you just leave."

As Katherine fled the bedroom, she realized how unusual her outburst was. She was shaking, and still energized by the rush of emotion. Shocking, she thought, that I would say such things. But it wasn't so difficult to smile and nod as she made her way to the bar. Somehow she had gained back her self-respect. Why did I wait so long to stand up for myself? she wondered, actually feeling quite triumphant in spite of her shock. As Lester approached her from behind the bar and smiled, she was affected, and wondered at how nice it seemed to have such a friend. "Would you fix me a drink?" she asked, concerned that the others could see her shaking. "Of course," Lester replied sympathetically. "Having a little problem with the Neanderthal man back there?" he whispered. Katherine smiled and nodded. Lester was her confidant. He knew her so well that he probably had figured out what happened. "Relax," he said helpfully. "You look beautiful. Don't let these petty domestic problems ruffle your feathers."

Margaret stroked her arm soothingly. She looked into the mirror, repeating the imagined 'Don't let these petty domestic problems ruffle your feathers . . .' She was pulling her head up high and admiring her own composure and appearance, when her eye caught his in the mirror. He stepped out of the shadow and smiled at her with a strange manner. Paul didn't say anything; he just stood there, leering at her. Margaret froze. Adrian will be home soon, she told herself. The statement gave her little comfort; it sounded too familiar. Anyway, she reasoned anxiously, the scientist will meet her. He can help.

A hostile Adrian stared at the liquor clerk. He was openly examining her, and taking his sweet time filling her order. Adrian was unaware that her height made the clerk concerned about the age factor. He didn't want to be arrested for selling to a minor. Little did he know how accustomed to dealing with life's ups and downs this young-looking being was. Finally he sold to the girl. Her clothes contradicted any possibility that she was undercover. As he pushed the big bottle at the small, angry snot, Adrian grabbed the half-gallon jug and turned, only to run into another ogling ogre.

Johann Hoffman was at a loss for words when the small woman he had been pursuing ran into him. He watched her interesting behavior, as engrossed as he had ever been. Never had he had such close contact with anyone quite so animalistic. As her eyes ran from his shoes to his head, the scientist wondered what he would say.

"What are you staring at, big cock?" Adrian demanded suspiciously. I'm surrounded, she thought angrily. Everybody's out to get me.

"Uhhhh . . ." Johann grunted oafishly. "I'm sorry," he finally uttered, his voice heavy with the German accent. "I wish I knew how to tell you."

Adrian knew an undercover dick when she saw one. They all wore those shiny black shoes. She had been expecting a raid for some time; business was going too good not to be troubled by payoffs. "You got something to say, copper?" Adrian snarled. "Spit it out."

The scientist didn't know where to begin. If he told her that there was a UFO on her roof, she would laugh in his face. On the other hand, he had to say something, because this creature was not going to listen to a detailed explanation. "You are in a dangerous position," he finally said.

"You guys will never catch me," Adrian answered contemptuously. I'm so clever, she congratulated herself. I've made arrangements to leave just in time. "Why are you so stupid, copper?" she queried suddenly. "Letting me know what's going down? That's really dumb."

Johann smiled at her in a "friendly American" way. He wanted to put her at ease. At least we're attempting to communicate, he thought uncomfortably. "What does it mean 'copper'?" he inquired in a "friendly" manner. "You misunderstand me."

Adrian seethed. I hate them, I hate them, she thought. I hate everything about them, especially their shiny black shoes. Enormous black shoes, she thought looking at his huge feet. Now this one is playing dumb. She felt like a cornered animal. There just wasn't enough room to move past the giant man. "Move out of my way," she demanded with authority. She really felt as helpless as a small child, like when the ones with the shiny shoes would take her poor drunken papa away.

"You don't understand," Johann insisted in a loud voice. He looked uncomfortably at the listening clerk. Johann felt that if he were to move, the girl would bolt out the door, and he would never catch her. But he didn't want to risk anyone hearing him talk of UFOs, especially if it didn't work out. If deaths occurred and the body of this small one should appear, the police might suspect him. "I can help you," the scientist implored in a stage whisper.

"Oh, I get it," Adrian said quickly. She knew a conspiratorial tone when she heard one. "You're a rat. You want me to put you on the take, in trade, you'll let me know when your little invasion is comin'."

"What?" Johann retorted in an excited tone. "Yes!" he said gleefully. "The invasion. What do you know about the invasion?"

The only thing Adrian hated worse than a cop was a crooked cop. "Shut your face, you stupid scab!" she exploded. "I don't play your way. I don't need you. I'm not giving you anything, so fuck off! Fuck off!" Adrian used the heavy bottle of vodka to knock him off balance so she could squeeze by. As she wiggled past him in panic, Adrian felt she had no one to turn to. She couldn't even confide in her girlfriend about what happened. Margaret would only reproach her about selling drugs.

Johann stood in confusion in the narrow store. He stared at the bottles of alcohol, and wondered what went wrong. There was a misunderstanding, that I know, he thought. But I really don't know what the little one said. I understood only half the words. Perplexed, he looked over the wine selection. He was pleased when he found his favorite brand. It was soothing to see a familiar item in such unfamiliar circumstances. He picked up the bottle, reading the label with pleasure. Here was something he could understand. It was, after all, in German.

It was the heat from his body that made her aware he was behind her. At first she didn't dare to look, she was so frightened. Margaret listened as he pulled the king's chair close and sat down in back of her. She was grateful for the size of both chairs. But when she looked into the mirror she saw that he had managed to get very close to her, by sitting on the arm of the chair. "Still sitting in front of the mirror, hmmm?" he said to her as she turned her head to examine his dirty-looking clothes and scraggy stubble. "Adrian isn't here," Margaret responded. She hoped that her intuition was wrong, and that he *had* come for a fix.

"I didn't come here to see Adrian," Paul said menacingly.

The way he smiled nauseated Margaret. She was ashamed. Ashamed that he was attracted to her. "Well, I don't have any dope for you. You'll have to see her about that," Margaret said in as snotty a voice as she could muster.

"I didn't come here for dope," Paul said lecherously. He reviewed her costume, blatantly looking for zippers and buttons.

As his eyes caressed her body, Margaret became angered. More sadistic than Paul to Margaret was Margaret to Margaret, for she loathed herself for his attraction to her. It's my fault, she blamed herself, that he's attracted to me. And now, she knew, she was going to get punished for it. "What do you want?" demanded Margaret, looking straight at the man.

"I came to help you gaze into the mirror," Paul said, smiling. "I know you like an audience, being a true narcissist."

Okay, thought Margaret, that's enough bullshit. I've been around enough to know when a creep is craving. "What do you want?" she repeated impatiently. Her voice dripped with loathing. She wasn't going to make it easy for him.

"To entertain you," Paul said calmly. He didn't have to remember what she looked like in the pink slip to get excited. Her breasts peeked out of the provocative purple gown. Paul could tell what kind of girl wanted it just by the way she dressed. He wasn't going to let her put him off.

"What makes you think I find you amusing?" said Margaret with a superior tone.

"I think I know what amuses you," retorted Paul.

This one smelled fear, so he came back, thought Margaret. The only way to deal with him is to show him I'm not afraid. Not hiding her disgust, Margaret said aggressively, "So how do *you* expect to entertain me?"

"The way men have always entertained women," he answered. He was angry now, and didn't try to hide it. This girl thinks she's smart, he thought. Superior bitches, they all think they're smart, even the whores. "I'm going to show you the difference between men and women," he threatened. This girl is no queer, he thought knowingly, and she needs a man to remind her of it.

"Don't make me laugh," Margaret barked contemptuously.

"I'm not going to make you laugh," Paul answered with a strained confidence. "I'm going to make you come."

"So what," growled Margaret. "I can come with or without you."

"Do you have something against a big, hard cock?" Paul pompously probes.

"If that's what I need I don't need you," Margaret remarked gleefully. "You're a junkie."

"You think I can't . . . get . . . it . . . up?" Paul threatened, rising to his feet.

"I don't care," Margaret remarked meekly. His self-assurance on the subject confused her. "When I want to fuck, I'll let someone else know about it, not you."

"I know you're wishing for a big, hard cock," he said ominously.

His hand reached over and the thick fingers pressed the skin near her collarbone. She was too frightened to move, afraid that any action would provoke him to beat her. Quietly she told him, "It seems to me that too many men today are telling me what I want. What I'm wishing is," she stated very clearly, "that you would leave."

"What are you gonna do if I stay?" Paul responds in a thick voice. His hand travels lower on Margaret's chest. "You can't call the cops. They'd love a chance to get in here."

Trapped! Margaret thought, before the words shot out of her mouth. "You think that's sexy!?" she shouted. "You think I'm turned on by that?" The thought of sex with the drug addict revolted her. "You make me sick, you wimpy junkie," she said, panicked and hopeless.

How could she call me names? thought Paul as he responded. "You're just a dyke," he said condescendingly.

"You're so attractive to me I'm just coming and coming," Margaret said sarcastically.

"Shut up, cunt. You're not coming yet," Paul spit. "I'm gonna fuck you till you know what it means, dyke."

"You sick pig," Margaret responded. "I don't need your cock for anything. You're a nothing," she barked hopelessly. "You're nothing. You're nothing."

With his fragile self-image, the mixed-up man couldn't take the insult. Paul snaps. Reaching forward, he rips open the delicate dress. Lace-covered buttons jump off Margaret onto the floor as if deserting a vessel. "You'll be sorry, you whore," Paul calls as he bullies her, pushing her up and into the center of the room.

His hands on her arms, the rough push and pull: it was more than enough for the other recent attacks to come dancing through her brain. A depository for semen, that's what I am, she thought, incredulous. "You're right," bellowed Margaret in a new voice, "I'm a whore." She ripped her own dress again, enlarging the previous tear. Then, pulling him toward the bed, she shouted, "Here!" with her eyes gleaming. "I'll lay down and you'll fuck me, see?" She pantomimed lying on the bed with her legs spread. "I don't care!" she said happily, looking like a crazy person. "It's not important to me whether *you* fuck me or not. Because you're just a fly. You don't exist."

Somewhere in her soul Margaret must have believed that Paul would be frightened off by her turning the tables. Because when he reached down to pull her dress open, Margaret tried to stop him. It was subtle. Only for a moment did she resist. There's no reason to get beat up again, she warned herself caustically. Anyway he's gonna end up squirting his load into me. She lay back and let him do it. Big deal! she told herself. And tried not to acknowledge his hands pawing her flesh.

After Johann had left, a bored Sylvia had thought about turning on the tube. Then she had realized there was something better to watch. Sitting at the telescope she could see the man rubbing his hands over the long torso of the blond girl. Immediately, Sylvia got excited. It had been a long time since she had any sex, and she wasn't going to miss this effortless opportunity for foreplay. She licked her lips with excitement and anticipation. Then the doorbell rang. Now I am going to fuck this giant, a determined Sylvia decided, as she moved toward the door. Preparing herself, she checked her appearance in the hall mirror and smoothed her garment before opening the portal to her prince.

Nothing could have been more disappointing to Sylvia than the sight of the Chinese man standing before her. I miss out on everything, she thought, and then she realized, I'm missing the activity in the punk apartment! Leaving the deliveryman standing in the doorway, Sylvia rushes back to the telescope.

Luxuriously, Sylvia sits, enjoying each sensual detail. She moves the shaft of the telescope deliberately, and refocuses the lens, just for the pleasure of it. Just as she is about to steal a peek at the pornographic pair, the delivery man reminds her of his presence.

"Are you studying stars, Miss Sylvia?" he interrupts. It wasn't the first time he had delivered food to the strange woman. She was one of the few customers that had an account with their company.

"Exactly," Sylvia answers automatically, not wanting to be disturbed from her pleasure. "Thank you," she calls, dismissing the dallier. As she finally peeks at the perpetrators, Sylvia calls out: "Oh my God!"

I've missed a lot, she realized. Already the pair were fornicating, but the Chinese didn't leave. "God, Miss Sylvia?" he persisted.

"God?" she asked, perplexed. Oh, he wants a tip! she realized. I've spoiled them by overtipping, she decided. "Add fifteen percent," she ordered.

"Very good," he called coyly as he moved slowly toward the door. "Thank you," the deliveryman said to the normally friendly woman, as he paused to watch her watch.

Sylvia stopped her observation and turned to glare at the caustic Chinese. "Thank you," she said politely, hiding her frustration when he didn't depart. "Bye-bye," she continued, hurrying his exit.

"Bye-bye", the Chinese said as he smiled and waved.

Still he didn't seem to move. Sylvia's pleasant demeanor slipped from her face. Quickly, the deliveryman responded to her glare. Sylvia sighed with relief when the bothersome boy finally shut the door behind him. I thought he would never leave, she said to herself, flabbergasted.

As soon as Sylvia looked through the telescope again, Margaret instantly became aware of the barrage of insults issuing forth from Paul's stinking mouth.

"I'll show you who doesn't exist. I'll show you, you whore," Paul berated the blonde. "You call me a junkie?" He waxed triumphant, his phallus securely sequestered in her tight channel. "You like my dope dick, whore. You like it because I can fuck you forever. You sit and wait for me to fuck you." She had been still and quiet for so long, as if in a trance, that Paul was surprised when she answered.

"I'm falling asleep," Margaret retaliated. She realized had made it too easy for him for too long. "Please hurry, because I'm tired and I'm falling asleep. You're boring me to death!" she spit, losing her cool at the end. The thought that the junkie would go on and on panicked her.

"Don't die," he answered, as if it was absolutely average love play. "You like it. You love it."

"Hurry up, please," Margaret said hysterically.

"What's your hurry?" answered Paul, pleased. "You like it. You love it."

Why aren't I tighter? Margaret panicked. How come he gained access to me so readily? She couldn't remember how it happened that he entered her. The guilt was too much to bear. "Fuck you," she cried crazily.

"I *am* fucking you," Paul yelled at her lustfully. "Fucking you," he repeated with relish. "I fuck you. Fuck you. Fuck you. Fuck. Fuck." With each stroke he cursed her and brought himself to new plateaus of excitement.

When Margaret could stand it no more, her thoughts turned to the alien. Immediately she was overwhelmed with excitement. Instantly she was close to coming. I'm gonna kill him, she thought in a wet, frenzied state. The alien's gonna knock him off like he, no, It, did before. Kill him dead, she repeated to herself, bringing herself closer to climax. I hate him, the alien likes me, he's jealous. He has no body and wants me totally. It wants me to be his, and his alone. It watches me fucking, likes my body, watches me, wants me. It will kill him. We will kill him. Kill him dead. Yes, yes, she ranted in her mind. Paul stopped moving, finished with his chore. But Margaret continued in her mind; she could see Sylvia watching. Witnessing the alien's love for her. She will see the death, and know I belong to another, Margaret assumed. As her climax came she found her pleasure in his death. But Sylvia wasn't watching. She was answering the door, going to her knight, thought Margaret. Now he's dead, thought Margaret, disgusted. Horrified, she pulled herself out from under his heavy, stinking body. Margaret moved slowly to the doorway, and walked out into the night. She knew the glass arrow was embedded in his head. But Margaret wanted more. "Hey, you!" she called out to the sky. "Hey, you. What's with these glass arrows? Who are you? Why are you killing these people here?" Margaret demanded. She needed proof. Proof that he cared for her. Evidence of Its infatuation. "Why are you killing these people here? I can't have these corpses here, these dead people. Please, no more corpses here. I don't want these bodies. No more bodies."

Margaret couldn't stand the thought of another dead man to haunt her. Owen's body was evidence. Proof of her failure to love him enough, proof of her guilt. Frightened, she turned to review the results of her anger and failure. Instantly the bulky form of Paul transformed into a foil statue—Silver ashes, thought Margaret with wonder— which crumpled into smaller and smaller sizes until it disappeared completely. Margaret was euphoric with relief. No one had ever done anything so nice for her. Thank you, she thought gratefully. Thank you. She wanted to do something good for It as well. "You did it for me, chief," she called in a wave of relief. "Why?" she flirted coyly. "Why don't you come out?" Margaret called to the sky in her sexiest voice. "Please come to me."

Paul hadn't moved after expelling his juice. Sadistically he made the bitch crawl out from under his inert body. It gave him almost as much pleasure as sex itself, to feel her struggling with panic to get out from under his weight. Her crazy cry to the sky interrupted the most pleasant of thoughts. He had been so content, until he realized that the bitch had freaked out. Quickly, he pulled up his pants and got the hell out of there. He realized that if from her rantings Adrian figured out what had happened, he was a dead duck. She could OD him at any time. Shit, he thought, I'll have to get a new supplier. The situation presented other surprise problems. He hadn't expected to have to wrestle with his conscience about this one. After all, she was a whore. You could see it by the way she dressed and painted her face. But her plaintive cries to the sky echoed in his head, even as he descended the stairs. I need a fix, he decided. That will "fix" it, he thought. And was amused by his own joke.

If Sylvia had not been so aroused by her watching, she could have found humor in the vision presented to her as she opened the door. A sheepish scientist stood, holding a bag open, offering its contents to the hostess. "I'm sorry to make you wait," the large man said, with his head bowed.

"It was my pleasure," Sylvia said ironically, as she led him into the kitchen. She wasn't going to acknowledge his gift right away, even if the wine was the perfect present. "How was your meeting with the girl?" she inquired courteously.

"She did not believe me," Johann replied sadly.

"Who would believe a man . . ." said Sylvia wittily, ". . . who is capable of waiting till the shrimps get cold?"

It seemed to Johann that she referred to more than food with her entertaining remark, but he couldn't concentrate. Anyway he knew the humor to be over his head, so he didn't attempt a response. He thought obsessively of his research. Johann wondered what had happened in his absence. When he could control his curiosity no longer, he began to follow his longing stare to the window. Then she acknowledged his gift.

"What have you got there?" said Sylvia. She knew he had gotten distracted by his "duty." This time he's not going to get away, she thought slyly.

"This is for you . . ." the scientist mumbled. "This is what I drink," he said, obviously distracted. "I thought . . ."

"Well, open it," the woman interrupted demandingly. She handed him a silver corkscrew and set him to work. "Stargazing after dinner," she ordered as she took his coat. "I assume you're not going to start talking about your duty again?" she warned him.

Peeling the Vegetables

When Adrian arrived, she looked at the mute Margaret's blankly beautiful face and wondered at her seeming lack of thought. There doesn't seem to be anything going on in her mind, she thought as she gently opened the bag to reveal her purchases. "Look what I got you," Adrian said proudly, and pulled out the chicken. She placed the bird on Margaret's lap, provoking a response. The response she elicited from her blond baby was far from her expectations, the contrast between her sweet face and rotten mouth being so extreme.

"Are you gonna fuck him?" Margaret challenged, remembering Owen. "He's dead. He's beautiful."

"No, baby," Adrian replied, falsely cheerful. "You're playing house, not me. You fuck him. Get him real juicy"—

Adrian salivated—"put him in the oven, and then we'll fuck." Adrian knew what Margaret liked. "Hasn't that always cheered you up before? A good fuck?" she said aggressively. But Margaret didn't respond. Spaced out again, thought Adrian, irritated.

Never had Chinese take-out been so well dressed. Sylvia set a beautiful table. The candles flickered, casting a soft light. The place mats matched the napkins and felt fine to the touch. One hundred percent combed cotton, thought Margaret. And her china finally had the proper setting to show off its former glory.

As Johann proudly poured the Moselle, the neck of the bottle clinked the crystal glass, sending Sylvia into a girlish giggle. She was happy. Finally, she was entertaining a heterosexual male in her home. Simultaneously, without conferring, Sylvia and Johann got ready to toast. It could not have been more perfect for Sylvia. We connected without speaking, she thought breathlessly. "To the success of your project," toasted Sylvia. She knew it would please him greatly if she acknowledged his work. At the same time Johann spoke. "To a beautiful and perfect hostess," he said. He really appreciated the understanding Judin.

Margaret seemed to be spacing out again, so Adrian decided to give her something to keep her active. The small woman dumped the potatoes and carrots into the aluminum roasting pan she had purchased, ripped open the brown paper bag she had brought the loot in, and spread it over the Orlon bedcover. Adrian set the whole mess in front of Margaret, but she didn't seem to notice. Margaret just sat on the bed with her hand on the moist, raw chicken. So Adrian flicked open her switchblade, demonstratively chopped into the air near Margaret's face, and handed it to her girlfriend, pointing to the vegetables. Finally Margaret got the message and began to peel a vegetable. Adrian drank her vodka and watched, content, finally having set Margaret to work at a domestic task. Idle hands are the devil's tools, she thought sarcastically, amusing herself. Margaret blinked hard, and looked at the small woman before her. It wasn't that she didn't recognize Adrian—the face was completely familiar to her; she just didn't know how this woman could treat her like that. She was, after all, loved, completely and totally loved by her alien. So it was beneath to her to be treated in such a manner by such an aggressive and uncouth person. As she remembered who Adrian was, and how their relationship operated, a strong, strange refusal of what had gone before possessed her. Margaret was sure that everything should be different now. Now that he—no, It—loves me, she reckoned. People shouldn't treat me like this anymore. He—I mean It—is, the most powerful individual force on the planet. I don't have to take it anymore, she assured herself happily.

She continued to peel, however, in spite of her comforting revelation. Margaret was enjoying herself and didn't want to think about practical things. The change would take a lot of effort. She would fill Adrian in on the new development later. Anyway, what's the big deal, she rationalized. I'm better at kitchen work than her. Adrian would have to be taught what to do. It's easier and faster to do it myself, Margaret figured. She had to get back to her scientist.

"Drugs," the producer said in a conversational tone. "Everyone is always speaking about them. All the teenagers are doing them. Now you tell me that aliens are also interested in drugs—in heroin! It's simply fantastic."

Johann was formulating a response, but since he was a foreigner, that took time. Sylvia continued. "I have a son. But he's not interested in drugs. He studies English literature at the university," Sylvia said pretentiously. We aren't all barbarians in this country, she was thinking. Sylvia would have told Johann about Jimmy's modeling as well, but somehow she didn't think the scientist would be as impressed.

"It might seem strange that the alien is interested in heroin. But there could be a lot of reasons for that," Johann explained excitedly, talking about his favorite subject. "Because of the research of a few American scientists in the late seventies," he continued confidentially, "we now know there are special opiate receptors in the human brain."

He doesn't like children, Sylvia concluded. I mentioned my son and he changed the subject. Hoping he wouldn't hold her prolificacy against her, she smiled and flirted gaily, cursing herself, thinking, Why did I have to mention that I already have a son? From prior experience, she knew that men didn't like it. "Opiate receptors . . . ?" she slurred as she sucked on a rather large shrimp. She was attempting to arouse him, but the slurring really got her irritated. I always slur when I'm tired, she noted. People think I'm drunk when I'm not. It's because I have crooked teeth. It's much more difficult to have good pronunciation when you have a malocclusion.

Johann continued enthusiastically, "Heroin, codeine, morphine, all belong to the same chemical family, which is derived from the poppy."

Which reminds me, thought Sylvia, I have to go to the dentist.

"They call them opiates," Johann stated with gravity.

I simply can't put it off any longer, Sylvia agonized.

"So that's what they found, these Americans, that there are special receptors in the human brain to receive opiate molecules," he informed her in a conspiratorial tone.

I keep putting it off because of the expense, thought Sylvia, but I shouldn't put it off any longer. It will wind up costing me more. "What are these opiate receptors doing sitting around in the human brain?" teased Sylvia. "Waiting for someone to give them heroin?" she joked.

"Let's speculate!" Johann said. It wasn't something he had been taught to indulge in, speculation not being considered very scientific. But on this research project he had been forced to do a lot of it; and found that he rather enjoyed it. "Some physicians think there is a naturally occurring molecule with the same molecular structure as opiates that is already present in the human body."

"You mean," said Sylvia, amused, "opium occurs naturally in the human body?"

"Not opium," Johann said, enjoying his ability to correct her. "I said a similar molecule with similar properties. Opium users have said that the drug creates a similar feeling to what people feel during orgasm. This molecule could be what is released in the brain during orgasm."

"This is getting very interesting," interjected the tipsy tyrant. "So, what about orgasm?" she drawled, deliberately slowing the pace of the conversation.

If Johann had been brought up differently, he might have noticed Sylvia's slovenly state. But, not having had much social life outside of his work, he had only his family life to draw on. A little slurring at dinner was what he was accustomed to. So Sylvia's condition seemed perfectly normal to him. "I have a theory," he continued excitedly. "If all humans have in their brain some substantial process based on the opiate mechanism of action, then why can't there exist in the universe some other form of conscious life which depends on this mechanism even more? Which would attract these aliens to heroin."

Even though she was inebriated, Sylvia was no slouch. She pondered his proposal. "According to you," she slurred provocatively, "to humans as well during orgasm. So that means orgasms are dangerous?" said the sexually excited woman. She began to pour them each a brandy. This ought to get him going, she wagered.

The scientist stared at his savior. She really saved me, the German giant pondered. But I wonder what kind of mating behavior she is into, with all these strange references. First she mentions something about being Jewish, now she says sex is dangerous. It makes me nervous to think what she might be into, especially with the diseases rampant in the metropolis. I wonder how long I have to stay at the table before I can get back to my research, he thought, nervously looking at the new offering of alcohol. I can't drink any more without it clouding my judgment.

"But," Sylvia continued, slithering closer, "aren't you looking forward to danger, O my brave knight?" She loved teasing him, especially since he seemed so flustered by it.

Photo Session

Adrian rose from her lounging and incidentally nudged Margaret as she responded to a noise in the hall. "Yo!?" she called out into the stairwell. Her voice echoed in the cavernous entrance.

"It's Jimmy," came the plaintive reply. "It looks like he got some money for some stuff," Adrian commented casually, breaking the quiet. She waited for Margaret to make a crack about her criminal life, but no reproach issued forth. The girl is really a space cadet, thought Adrian disparagingly.

Neither girl was prepared for the onslaught of fashion followers that streamed into the apartment. A whole crowd of people entered their environment. Even social Adrian was momentarily overwhelmed. They carried clothes covered in plastic, makeup cases, lights, cameras, equipment, colored paper, and a collective curiosity about the residents of the bizarre penthouse. Jimmy was the first of the entourage to reach the pair on the bed, wearing the clinging photographer huddled over his right shoulder. Jimmy grimaced at the show of displayed domestic activities before him on the bed. He was embarrassed to be associated with peers involved in such bourgeois activities. He knew that Adrian couldn't be the cause of the food preparation; so his anger about his own embarrassment fell on Margaret, whose intricate makeup seemed to be crumbling off of her uncouth face.

Margaret looked up from her stupor in horror. The strangers were all staring at her, waiting for her to perform. Only she didn't know her lines, not even her character, so unprepared was she to be herself. Finally she recognized a familiar face, the photographer's manager, who had approached her at a fashion show, and remembered the arrangement another Margaret had made so long ago.

"I forgot," she said, panic-stricken, to the unresponsive photographer's manager, Jack. "I mean . . . I forgot time, the time . . ." she repeated anxiously. She felt so out of the world, Margaret didn't know if they could understand her, if her language was decipherable to them. But she did know that she couldn't do it, that there was no way she could play her part in the fashion happening. Margaret noticed the camera ominously dangling around the slimy photographer's neck. She felt they wanted to kill her with those cameras. Margaret knew it was ridiculous, but she had the feeling they wanted to capture the little bits of herself she had left by taking her image. Having her picture taken seemed, right now, to be an attack. "I'm not ready," she pleaded with the jaded Jack, as the photographer, slimy on the slim Jimmy, hurried to put the film in his Polaroid.

"Don't think about it," retorted the manager. Dealing with erratic egos was his job. He knew a malleable model when he saw one. "That's what their job is," he assured his asset. "They are going to fix you up beautifully," Jack said as he dismissed her self-doubt.

The photographer, standing so close to his infatuation, could feel Jimmy's disdain at the housework displayed. Wanting to please his paramour, the excited artist interjected sarcastically, "Don't move! I love it! The chicken is great. Let me get a shot."

The following flashes made it difficult to see. Spots appeared in the air before Margaret's alarmed eyes. The alien is not going to like this! the blonde told herself bravely.

"What do ya' think you're doing?" an alarmed Adrian snapped. "You can't go around snappin' pictures of people when they're not ready!" It wasn't that she was defending her girlfriend. She was sitting too close to her. Adrian happened to get in Margaret's spotlight and wasn't accustomed to being treated so disrespectfully.

A formidable woman with an authoritative voice answered Adrian's anger. "Calm down, children," the clothing designer commanded. "I've got some cocaine for you and I don't want any squabbling. We are going to have a marvelous time," she ordered.

"Margaret, this is Nellie," the photographer sniffled. As soon as Jimmy departed the area with a sneer, the photographer became human. It wasn't in Brian's nature to be cool. He had affected the behavior to impress his infatuation. Brian had a letch for Jimmy of monumental proportions. "She's the fashion editor for *Midnight Magazine*," the photographer whispered excitedly. He presented her as his experience warranted, his nose already brown from selling himself to fickle fashion editors. This was press with a capital P. Adrian, lying with her lover on the bed, couldn't help

but compete. Her anger at Margaret for ignoring her earlier was still fresh. She was a little more diplomatic than the
dumbstruck Margaret and knew a potential plug when she
saw one. She looked over the tall, shapely writer and interjected appreciatively, "She has longer legs than yours,
hasn't she Margaret?"

The fifties-style rock-a-billy redhead Adrian referred to
professionally pushed the portable tape player under Margaret's nose. "You don't mind, do you," she presumptuously began. "I would like to ask you a few questions,"
the reporter continued.

"No, no," Margaret responded. "Not now."

"Margaret!" Jack interrupted. "What are you doing?" It
was irritating to him that the New Waver would take her
style so seriously as to reject the publicity he had arranged.

"Turn it off!" Margaret demanded. "Now!"

"If she doesn't want," said the redheaded reporter, "she
doesn't want." There are plenty of Club personalities who
want promotion, thought the attractive writer. But another
voice in her head disagreed. Nellie smelled a story. The
rejection intrigued her in spite of her savvy. The reporter
went out to the roof to think and get away from the crowd.
It took her a while to move through the stylists readying the
clothes, the makeup artist setting out his paints, the hair
stylist arranging her hairbrushes, before she could break
out onto the uncrowded roof. The view was something to
behold—a panorama of skyscrapers and lights. A photographer's assistant interrupted his work and stood beside her,
also awed by the city. "Brian was right. This roof is perfect," he said to her, wanting to share the moment. Nellie
hardly heard him. Somehow the view encouraged her to be
more aggressive in capturing this chapter in nightlife.
"This fucking city is really something," she said emphatically.

"Drugs?!" demanded Jimmy of Jack. He knew his rights. The hair person was waiting patiently to start Jimmy's treatment, but the tired twin wasn't letting her do her duty before he knew about the supply. "Be patient," Jack said, bored, as he looked for a match to light the jaded Jimmy's held-out cigarette. "Light," the brat boomed at his hairdresser. She gave him a look of warning. It was a rude way to start the session. They hadn't even said hello yet.

"Margaret, come here," the makeup man whined impatiently. He stood next to Margaret's antique chair, waiting for its owner to occupy it. Margaret was hurt that Adrian was paying so much attention to the redheaded reporter. She doesn't want me, the blonde agonized. With the room full of strangers, the most comforting place for Margaret to be, it seemed, was in her chair. So, Margaret left her lover, left her warm spot on the platform bed, and made her way to her favorite place. She walked as if in a daze. It would seem familiar to have them working on her, she knew. There would be comfort in the brushes moving on her face.

The photographer's manager sighed with relief when the model sat down to be made up. He hadn't been sure of her participation until then. She had seemed unwilling to accept her occupation. Jack poured himself a congratulatory drink from Adrian's half gallon of alcohol. He had brought all the artists together, and they were busy with their creative tasks. His work was over; the rest was up to them.

"What have you done to yourself now, Margaret?" the makeup man cried when he saw the purple and pink painted tears dripping down her delicate skin. She was always wearing that heavy acrylic intricately patterned on her light skin. He wondered that her complexion was so clear with all the abuse. But mostly he resented her artistic efforts, being an artist himself. The paint was peeling after her encounter with Paul, and she did indeed look unkempt.

"She can't hide it," the jaded Jimmy called from the opposite wall. "A chicken is a chicken."

Jimmy's hairdresser was determined to put him in his place before he started abusing her, too. "Come on, Jimmy," she corrected him. "You're both so beautiful, and you look alike. Be nice!" she commanded.

"I'm not a chicken," the junkie insulted his modeling mate. "Ouch," he called out, as the hairdresser pulled deliberately at his bleached-blond locks.

"I'm sorry Jimmy," she said sarcastically. "I didn't realize your scalp was so sensitive." It was untrue. She knew his roots burned at every bleaching because she completed the task herself. He would understand her deceit was deliberate.

The frighteningly authoritative voice of the designer rang out over the racket in the apartment. She was organizing the collection, deciding the order of outfits to be photographed, and keeping her helpers in line. "Don't get anything dirty, and tape the tags to the inside. It's not necessary to cut them."

The stylists looked at each other in distaste. What they had thought was going to be a fun, creative task, was turning into slave labor. "Where's the cocaine?" the stylist, Nancy, demanded in response. I'm not going to work without the promised perks. I want to have some fun, she decided.

"David?" the formidable fashion maven called out to her much younger lover. "Would you fix us a few lines, dear?" The cheerful young man nodded his head happily. Of course he was ready for candy. He always was.

"I've got some blow too, baby," Jack interjected. He liked the cheerful, good-looking boyfriend of the designer too, and knew how to impress him. "Here," he said, tossing the large bag of cocaine to the attractive boy. Everyone tried not to notice the large bag flying through the air, but it was just too large an amount of snow not to warrant some open mouths. Everyone suddenly worked faster, knowing that soon they would want to be unoccupied so they could enjoy their portion of powder. David put on appropriately avant-garde music, and adeptly set up a series of the long white lines on a large tray. Adrian's big bottle of vodka traveled the room, loosening everyone up, and inspiring liberal use of the popular powder. Photographer's assistants scurried around setting up lights and searching for outlets and they created a general feeling of excitement. Everyone felt uplifted. The party began.

There was the feeling that they were going to create something special, something new, something never done before. And each person felt even more uplifted after their toot. As the second round of drug dispensing began, the lines on the tray had gotten considerably longer. Few present had seen this much cocaine before. Most were impressed. A nonverbal competition evolved as to who could take the most cocaine in one toot. When it was Jimmy's turn again, the master of minimal proved that he was maximal in something after all. His intake capacity was astounding. The workers were in awe of him once again. Here was a expert, they observed; he even snorted with gloves on.

By this time Margaret's makeup had progressed to a point where it became obviously interesting. The colors curled over her cheekbones bright over a white base. One eye peeked out of a gold and green bed of mystery, her blue eye rimmed in black. It was a delicate pattern of oddly Japanese inspiration which the makeup man painted on her now, less substantial than she normally painted herself, but more glamorous, more attractive, definitely in response to what she normally wore. The redheaded reporter watched with concealed interest. A little cocaine had made it difficult for her to leave the situation alone, as she had planned. Nellie had a multitude of questions for Margaret that were flooding her head, which had been stimulated by the drug. Maybe she will be more willing to speak, now that she has had some cocaine, thought the eager writer. She approached the model as the makeup man worked on her face. Margaret couldn't move. If she did, the makeup would end up in the wrong place on her face. So Nellie took advantage of her immobility, as any professional would. "I'd like to ask you a few questions about your childhood," she stated, overcome with curiosity.

Nobody would have guessed the relief that Margaret felt when Adrian answered the buxom Nellie from across the room. Many nights of Club life had instilled in Margaret the ability to hide her true feelings under a mask of hauteur. She got so good at her cover that she did it without thinking, almost to the point of not knowing her true reactions herself. Nellie was fascinated by the regal, unperturbed manner with which Margaret received her inquiry. But Nellie needed information foremost and didn't let Margaret's glamour deter her from the task. This was a girl fully aware at all times of the bottom line.

"Come here, legs," Adrian called persuasively. "Can't you see she's busy? I'll tell you all about her childhood." As the reporter approached, Adrian eagerly pulled a portfolio of photos from under the bed.

When Nellie arrived, the lecherous lesbian had left a small space on the bed for her to sit. But the reporter's curiosity was stronger than her adverse reaction to Adrian's advances. She settled herself beside the small woman. Her surprise when she looked at the first of many snapshots and photographs was total. Before her was the face of a healthy, unpretentious young girl in a turtleneck. You could hardly recognize the bleached blonde as the same person in the pictures. This was the face of a small-town girl.

Meanwhile the party continued. They had dressed her now in one of the bright, strange outfits, and had begun shooting photographs in a frantic, wild fashion. As Jimmy and Margaret posed, everyone watched, while listening to the inspiring music. Only Adrian and Nellie looked at the pictures of the past.

"Margaret is from Connecticut," Adrian began. "She went to church every Sunday," the singer stated proudly. "Look," she said, pointing to a large picture. "This is when she was sixteen."

A photography student in the small town where Margaret grew up had made her his subject in an almost obsessive way. The pictures were professional in their technical aspects, and naïve in their execution. The result was an accurate picture of a person willing to please. Her smiles were radiant, her enthusiasm real. Too inexperienced to pose professionally, the girl had simply been herself. So there were many photographs of the girl in her teen years. In some she wore bathing suits, the awakening of her sexual identity clumsily recorded; in some she was still a child; they covered a range of years until the girl left home for college. Those, and the family photographs of certain occasions, gave an unusually complete picture of the life of this person. Nellie did not understand why she became so upset alternatively watching Margaret model and looking over the album. She needed to understand why the portrait of Margaret's development made her so very sad.

Everybody wanted to be involved in creating the new style for the eighties. Consumed with passion for their work, stimulated by the drug, they took turns putting things on their subject and taking them off. Margaret remained passive throughout, as was her job and habit to do.

An eager stylist put a feather in the passive poser's do. The hairperson became immediately enraged. "What are you doing?" she demanded theatrically. "This is my hair. You can at least consult me about it."

"I think, Jane," the designer interjected, "that the hair-dresser . . ."

"Hair stylist!" the enraged worker fumed.

"Hair stylist," the designer conceded, "is right," she continued diplomatically. "We don't need this accessory. The image should be sssim-ple."

The designer settled the dispute before it could escalate. But the general feeling was that, with all the energy being released, tempers would flare and that all would be entertained.

Simple! thought Nellie, observing the mayhem. This look is anything but simple. The resulting fashion looked like an imagination had run amok. Colors were the brightest ever, cut with black in large bands, the makeup as memorable as the costumes. And make no mistake about it, these were costumes. Not a single outfit could be worn without attracting attention. These were compilations of comment, not necessity. They were made to say something about the time that we live in, Nellie decided.

The session progressed at a more professional pace now. As the artists came off their drug, their minds wandered. The photography session started to feel like work. Standing on the tables, high above the heads of the others, Jimmy felt the loss of awe for what was happening. He had liked being above the crowd on the makeshift runway. Being the center of attention made him feel wanted. It made him feel powerful. They were doing doubles. He had been posing with passive Margaret when their attention waned. Panicked, he felt the pressure to perform. So, at the most inopportune times, he would delight in demeaning Margaret. Sometimes he whispered insults in her ear as they were posing perfectly together. Sometimes he responded by pushing her, or pulling on her clothes in a juvenile fashion. The workers responded well. The abuse of his co-worker seemed to hold their attention. During all of this, the durable Margaret remained passive. She was soothed by the familiar flashes and paralyzed by her position. She didn't want any trouble; she was afraid a commotion might make the UFO fly away. So Margaret kept thinking, through all the humiliation, that it didn't matter. Because soon, the shoot would be over and she would be with her alien.

But it wasn't over. Each time they moved her inside to remove the makeup, Margaret believed they were through. Then another coat of white would be sponged onto her face, as though it were a canvas. But Margaret accepted her work dutifully; the idea of stopping the flood of attention never occurred to her. She was a model. Every girl in America would love to be in her position. And she was their choice. After all, with that there went a responsibility.

This is the face of a small-town girl who believes the best is yet to come, thought Nellie sadly, looking at Margaret's earlier images. How did she get like this? the reporter wondered, looking at the "creative" posing in the bizarre costumes. What could be going on in her mind? When she could contain her curiosity no longer, Nellie again crossed the room to where they were painting Margaret and began questioning her.

"Your photographs that Adrian was just showing me indicate a fairly traditional upbringing. What do you mean by all this weird makeup and strange clothes?"

"Nothing," said Margaret in a quiet rebuttal. She hated the redhead with the large mouth. She wished she would go away and leave her alone like the others.

She can't believe this is just a fashion, thought Nellie

anxiously. How can she think that Seventh Avenue would reproduce this weird style? "It's tacky," claimed the reporter provokingly.

The critical word echoed in Margaret's head. "You're tacky," she retorted to the reporter. The first thing you learned in Club life was to keep your mouth shut. The redhead was not one of them or she would understand. It's all before her if she wants to know, thought Margaret contemptuously. All she has to do is look.

"What do you mean by all this weird makeup and strange clothes?" repeated the reporter.

"Nothing," said Margaret. Some things are beyond words, but you wouldn't understand that, because you have no grace, she thought, returning the redhead's gaze.

"You don't admit to dressing strange?" Nellie continued.

How can she keep asking me these stupid questions in front of all these people? thought the model. The word "strange" echoed in her head. Somewhere, long ago, they had called her that before. And the pain of it haunted her. Suddenly, she wasn't sure of the others. The group seemed against her. "You're strange," she spit defensively.

Now I'm getting somewhere, the reporter thought, excited. Eagerly she continued her inquiry, not wanting to lose the pace. "What do you mean by that? I'm not wearing socks of two different colors."

It was Adrian who answered, unintentionally saving Margaret from her personal persecution. "You're wearing what they want from you . . . baby," she taunted, wanting attention from the redhead.

"Who they?" demanded the demonstrative damsel. A lot of innuendo, but no explanations, thought the bottom-line dame.

Jack shouted with abandon, his shape soggy with alcohol. "America!" he sang, still elegant in spite of his intake.

Adrian couldn't stand being on the sidelines. This dramatic opportunity could not go unexploited by her. She took the position of the provocateur even though she understood exactly what Jack meant. "What do you mean, America?" she stated grandly. "I'm American." The small woman pointed a short finger at her tall girlfriend. "She is American." Adrian loved to feel her blood boil. "He is American," Adrian angrily explained, pointing at Jimmy. We are as much a part of this society as any of them, she thought, self-righteously agitated. "Where are you from?" she continued provocatively, pointing at one of the stylists. "Massachusetts," answered the smiling assistant, pleased to have been included in the entertaining display. Adrian points to each person and they, in turn, call out enthusiastically the place where they are from. "Denver." "Tennessee." "Detroit." "Ohio." "Florida." "Portland." Places from across the land bounce off the walls of the narrow room. Triumphant, Adrian suggests smugly, "You see? All the country is represented here."

"Right." A sarcastic jeer from Jimmy cuts through Adrian's satisfaction. He continues with her thesis to make it sound preposterous. "And this chicken"—he refers to Margaret—"is the Miss America of the eighties." "No, Jimmy," answers Adrian wisely, "you are." She continued her barb by singing the coronation song of the TV nation. "Here he is . . . Miss America . . ." With the joke, the whole group joins in, singing the familiar song, wanting to share in the hilarity. "No," said the designer pointedly, interrupting the chorus, "I think Margaret is Ms. America." "No, I think it's Jimmy," the photographer interjected. "You just say that because you're gay," his manager chided him. "He's not gay all the time," the stylist Nancy informed the group with a giggle.

"I seriously think Jimmy is the new Ms. America. He has

all the mannerisms of a sex symbol," the photographer insisted. "That's what we should call this. Make it a series, 'The two Ms. Americas,' " Jack aided his artist. "That's a great idea!" the assistant assisted the photographer. Fed by his underling's enthusiasm, Brian gets a brainstorm. "And we can end it with the two of them fucking," the photographer exclaims.

Fucking again? thought Margaret, bewildered. Then, suddenly, she was enraged. "He can't fuck," she said sadistically, attacking her proposed tormentor.

"I can too fuck," answered Jimmy jocularly. "I just can't fuck you."

"You two are just too chicken to be photographed fucking," Adrian interjected.

"Chicken woman," Jimmy called his unappealing associate.

"He's the chicken, not I," Margaret triumphantly answered the group.

"That sounds like a challenge to me, Jimmy," Jack encouraged the boy.

"You look like a chicken," Jimmy jeered at Margaret.

Margaret could see where this competition was headed, and she was sorry for her impulsive anger. He knows not what he does, she thought anxiously. "Please Jimmy," she tried to warn him. "Don't start on me now."

"You look tired," Jimmy pressed on, momentarily pretending to be concerned for her. "You look old, and ugly, and washed up," he said, harassing her. Then he observed her and waited gleefully for her reaction.

"OOhhh!" the assistants called. They wanted to be involved too. "Go to it!" they said, excited.

"Don't talk to her like that," the designer said prudently, halfheartedly scolding Jimmy. "We still have two rolls of film." She had invested a lot of energy in the endeavor and wanted to make sure that she would get the best possible results.

"Stop it, Jimmy." Margaret tried to talk to the barbarous boy. The alien will kill him if he continues, Margaret thought sadly. "You don't understand anything," she said, exasperated.

"What I don't understand," Jimmy jeered happily, "is why anyone would want to take your picture. That's what I don't understand." The crowd reacted favorably to his joke, and Jimmy was pleased. I'm not like her, he told himself emphatically. For a phrase his voice carried a hint of hysteria. "You're just a freak," he said too loudly. "A weirdo," he continued coolly. "Behind your back everyone laughs at you. They call you chicken woman."

"That's why you look just like her," the hairdresser reminded him.

Jimmy was taken aback by the comment. Not knowing what to say, he impulsively stepped on Margaret's painted toe. It was sticking out the tip of the red high-heeled shoe. As his booted foot came down on it, Margaret repressed her cry of pain. I'm not going to give him the satisfaction, she thought, blocking the sensation.

"Don't step on that shoe," the designer ordered. "We'll have to pay for it."

"Chicken woman. Chicken woman," Jimmy said. He seemed to rant for a moment, then he calmly recited, "One day the chicken woman had chicks, and everyone stepped on them, because they were so ugly. Cluck, cluck," he called.

The hair stylist and the makeup artist looked at each other. In a rare psychic moment, they burst into song. " 'Old McDonald had a farm, E . . . I . . . E . . . I . . . O. And, on this farm he had some chickens, E . . . I . . . E . . . I . . . O. With a chick, chick here and a chick,

chick there. Here a chick . . .' " they sang in hysteria, miming the action of stomping on a small bird " '. . . there a chick. Everywhere a chick, chick.' " Most joined in on the chorus, or called out, "Chick, chick." Soon there was a plethora of stomping, laughing, hysterical participants.

Only David, the designer's young boyfriend, remained inactive, a look of concern on his pretty face. "What's going on? What's going on? Why is everyone being so mean?" he called out.

The then laughing Nellie caught herself with his observation. What am I doing? she wondered, looking around herself at the hilarious people.

"Don't make me hate you," Margaret warned her adversary. He doesn't realize the power of the alien, she told herself. They're all laughing at me, but I hold true power, she reminded herself. The ability to kill.

"You are too old to model," Jimmy continued, unabashed. "Everyone talks about your famous bags. The biggest eye bags around. Chicken woman with the eye bags." Jimmy seldom laughed, but he did now. He was really enjoying himself. "You are so ugly . . ." he said to his co-worker.

"And you are so beautiful," Margaret interrupted. "The most beautiful boy in the world."

For a moment Jimmy didn't speak. He didn't know what to make of this turn in the events. "What?" he managed to utter at last. Maybe I misunderstood her, he thought.

Margaret came and stood right in front of him and continued her praise. "I don't care what you say. I can only love you," she said, staring into his face.

"Margaret . . . what's wrong with you?" came the concerned reply.

"Let me see your eyes," Margaret said with a sultry sadness.

"Oooooooooo," the crowd responded approvingly.

"God. What eyes," she said honestly. This is the way he wants it, she had decided. If he demands a public execution, he will get one, thought the model, who had always been eager to please.

"Chicken woman," Jimmy jeered angrily. I am not like her, he repeated in his mind. She's awful. Just awful.

"Come on, Jimmy," a boy called, encouraging his mentor.

"And your lips," Margaret said sexily, moving closer.

"Ooooooooo," the crowd responded eagerly.

"You are so old and ugly I can't look at you," Jimmy said defensively. He became very uncomfortable when the group seemed to favor Margaret's comments.

"Come on," called the hair stylist angrily. "She's beautiful."

"No," said Margaret, taunting Jimmy. "I know I'm unattractive. You should punish me. I'm not good enough for you. I'm just an old and ugly whore." It was the part of her that believed it that Jimmy responded to.

"The oldest and the ugliest," Jimmy quickly quipped.

"I'll be your whore. Do you want to beat me?" Margaret asked her cohort.

"Beat her! Beat her!" came the response from the frenzied group. "Move the lights," said Brian, punching his assistants into action. "Pay attention," he admonished them. "Quickly. Quickly."

"Yeah?" queried a confused Jimmy. "You want me to hit you?" There was a part of him that knew she needed punishing, and then there was the boy that dared not do it.

"Whatever you want, I'll do it," Margaret answered, urging him on. Kind of like last request, she thought to herself righteously.

"Yeah," jeered the crowd. "Do it. Come on. Do it."

Jimmy was panicked by the demands of his audience. He didn't know what to do. He looked at her bloodshot eyes and dark circles. She's a mess, he thought, repulsed. A young observer called to him lovingly, "Do it, do it." Sharply his gloved hand swung around and whacked her painted face. It felt good, he decided. The act was something clean, and clear to him.

The crowd went berserk. Margaret saw stars. She was surprised that he had hit her so hard, he had seemed uncommitted to the act. Now he dies, thought Margaret, with her face stinging. "You are so beautiful, and I am so ugly," she said to him, trying to conceal her anger. "I think you should hit me. Hit me! Hit me!" she cried.

Jimmy obliged the model and the masses by striking her several times. He remembered why he was hitting her and called out, "You ugly old whore."

"Do it again," came the response from the crowd. His hand stopped in midair when he heard *her* words.

"Let me suck your beautiful cock. Let me do it for you. You can beat me if I do it wrong." It was a turn in events Jimmy hadn't expected.

Here was something Margaret knew how to do. Long ago they had taught her, along with how to kiss. Later on, she had been surprised when the movie *Deep Throat* had made such a big deal out of it. Margaret had always assumed all women knew how to do it. She had gotten very good at pushing a phallus to the back of her throat to open the mouth of her esophagus. With a lot of pressure it would open up, like when you have a baby. Of course it hurt. The tears would come to her eyes, but at least she could breathe. The only real danger was choking as it erupted. She would always try to trick them by pulling it away from her breathing passage before they erupted it. But her first boyfriend always could tell. They said she was very good at it. That she gave them pleasure. It would always arouse her, but then she would be left all alone with her desire. Margaret knew that it was the fastest way to get them off. When she was young, she had been very concerned at relieving their pain as quickly as possible.

She heard Brian call for some light for their faces as she unzipped his fly. Anyway, they aren't gonna see my face, she thought to herself. When she looked at Jimmy, for a moment she thought he looked frightened. But then he said, "Beg for it," in the familiar, aggressive way, and she dismissed the thought. "Beg for it, Margaret," she thought she heard the crowd jeer. And then he kicked her, and a sharp pain ran up her leg.

Suddenly everything seemed different to her. "You asked for it," she said confidently. That's the last time anyone will ever hurt me, she swore to herself, and she slipped gracefully to her knees.

She rubbed her face calmly on his flaccid phallus. She had seen worse cases than that. It never occurred to her that they wouldn't complete the act. "I want your cock, baby. Please let me," she called to him and all who cared to listen. "I'll do it good, baby," she promised him. "You can beat me if I do it wrong." After all, she knew what they liked.

"I can't," Jimmy answered softly. For a split second sympathy passed between them as he realized that she was like him. That they were the same, just doing what they were expected to do. We share the same sad life, he thought, in wonder. But the faces looking at him haunted him. They were waiting. Waiting for him to perform with her. And it was her fault. She put him in the position of having to. "Come on, Jimmy, do it!" came the adoring cry from the young lips of the photographer's assistant. Then Jack, holding the mirror to flash light in their faces called, "Look at yourself."

And he did. Jimmy liked what he saw. I don't look like her, he decided. I look good. I look great. She is shit and I am beautiful, he thought, and his cock swelled full. And she sucked it well, as a whore should, as he looked at his own great, handsome face.

"Look at yourself," Jack's soothing voice called to him. "You are the most beautiful boy. You are the most beautiful fucker. We want to see you fuck her."

"Fuck her, fuck her," called the crowd. "Do it. Do it," they cheered him. Jimmy loved the attention. Margaret's continued skill was the other mitigating factor, and there was no doubt of her ability, he decided. But what else could be expected, he thought sadistically, she is a dirty whore. "You whore," he cursed her. They will all admire as I blast off, he thought, excited.

"Don't soil that garment, Margaret," the designer told the model. These are, after all, my samples. I have to use them again, the fashion maven thought, concerned.

"Get him, Margaret, you whore," Adrian called to her from far away. Margaret did as she was told. She did a great job of sucking him, as good as she knew how. Jimmy's voice got lower as he cursed her. It started to come from a deeper place. "Do it right, you ugly chicken. Do it good, you whore. You old whore. You whore." His member trembled slightly as he repeated himself. But she didn't pull away. She let him come full in her throat, not sure if she would be able to breathe.

She struggled with the sticky residue in her throat. As she finally caught some air, she realized he was gone. The alien has killed him, she thought. But her struggle for breath made her uninterested in witnessing his disappearance. When Margaret could breathe again, the faces were gathered around her, aghast with shock. What did you expect? she thought, feeling attacked by their strange expressions. "You made me do it," she quietly accused them. "This pussy has teeth," she confessed softly. "No one should fuck me ever."

Adrian moved toward her from out of the crowd. She stood over her kneeling girlfriend with the heavy head. She wanted Margaret to repeat what she had uttered earlier. "What did you do with him, Margaret?" she demanded.

"I killed him," Margaret answered, surprised. She looked around her at the sullen faces. Isn't it obvious? she thought.

"Where's his body?" Adrian asked angrily.

What's she mad at me for? thought Margaret, confused. "I don't know," she answered irritably.

"Someone look over the edge," ordered Adrian sarcastically. A smiling stylist gladly proceeded to the open roof. She mimed looking over the edge and shouted, "There's nothing out here," to the quiet crew. Still no one seemed to see the humor in the situation, so the stylist made a crack. Pointing to a large cardboard carton, she commented, "What's in the box?" Continuing with irony, she joked, "Was this a magic trick?"

Nervously Adrian shared a glance with her frightened girlfriend. "No," she announced authoritatively. "This isn't a magic trick. I keep dead bodies in the box so I can fuck them." The laughter that followed had the effect of a pin in a balloon. The whole group relaxed and started moving around the room again. Margaret sighed with relief until Adrian's hand gripped her neck possessively. Margaret could feel Adrian's anger in her fingers. No! Margaret thought, moving away from her hand. I don't want it anymore. I don't want her anger. She doesn't understand, Margaret panicked. She can't do that to me anymore. Everything is different now. "You should stay away from me," she informed her miniature mate.

"What are you talkin' about?" Adrian said condescendingly. She grabbed her girlfriend. I'm not gonna let her reject me in front of all these people. Especially right after she sucked Jimmy off, Adrian thought, outraged.

"I killed him," Margaret said quietly.

Adrian knew about people acting crazy. Her mother had humiliated her many times in public. But I'm not a kid anymore, Adrian told herself. And I'm not gonna let this bitch get the best of me in front of all these potential clients. I know how to handle her, she realized, remembering her mother's freak-outs before the loony bin. You just got to play along with them, she decided. "How?" Adrian asked, patronizing her spouse.

"I kill all the people that fuck me," the model answered earnestly. "That's it. If you fuck me, you'll die."

"Come off it, Margaret," Adrian snapped nervously. She has really flipped, she thought, sickened.

"No. It's true," insisted Margaret. "I'm serious," she said, thinking, Abso-fucking-lutely serious, just like Paul.

"Of course you are," Adrian patronized her friend. I hate her, thought Adrian. Always makin' a fool of me. I'll show her. In a ringmaster voice she continued. "Who wants to take bets on this?" she asked happily. "Who thinks I can fuck Margaret and not die?"

The photographer wasn't impressed. He didn't have any film left anyway. "It's too much, Adrian, lay off. There's something very strange going on here. I'm going to leave."

"Sure there's something strange," Adrian agreed. "I'll bet you three hundred dollars that I can fuck Margaret and not die."

"Of course you won't die," said the photographer, amused. "But I don't know if watching you two fuck is worth three hundred dollars." Brian had been sorely disappointed when Jimmy had left. He knew he might find him at the Club. But he had spent more than one evening trying to get the attention of the difficult boy. Jimmy had never seemed to notice him. It irked him that the dyke Margaret got closer to Jimmy than he did. I really hate her, he decided. "It sure sounds interesting, I'd like to watch," he said, debating which activity would be more amusing, hunting for Jimmy or watching them. Then he realized that Margaret didn't want to participate. "But I'm not sure Margaret is in the mood," he said, his realization in his voice.

"Adrian, you should stay away from me," Margaret pleaded, seeing in what direction the events were leading. "I'm a killer," she tried to convince her girlfriend.

"Come on, baby," the angry Adrian spit as she pulled her girlfriend across the floor. "You like to fuck. You like to fuck better than anything."

"I don't want you," Margaret said softly, trying to reason with her irate friend.

"Why not?" answered Adrian angrily.

"Because I am killing all the people I fuck," Margaret stated clearly.

"You kill me? You kill me?" Adrian demonstratively cried to her audience. "That's the joke of all time."

Margaret could see now that she wasn't going to get off the hook by reasoning with her girlfriend. She struggled to loosen the hold Adrian had on her arm. But when Margaret tried to get to her feet, her agile adversary pulled her toward the bed. "Leave me alone," Margaret pleaded as she was pulled. Adrian answered, "You like it. You like it." Margaret remembered Paul. Just like Paul, she said to herself, and let her girlfriend force her down on the bed. He said, you like my dope dick, whore. And now he's dead, she told herself.

Adrian straddled her diagonally, their parts pressed to-gether. She pushed Margaret's long leg high and rested it on her own shoulder. It never took Adrian much effort to get excited. All she had to do was to look at one of Marga-ret's long legs and she was halfway there.

"Don't do it," Margaret said. She felt obliged to try to stop her girlfriend from causing her certain death. But it was hard to care, it seemed so hopeless to her.

"I always get what I want," Adrian reminded her crazy friend as she moved on top of her. She needs to be pun-ished, Adrian thought, excited. And now I'm gonna fuck her good. "These good people want to see me fuck you," she said, moving sharply as she said the dirty word. "So you are gonna get fucked." With the clean movement on the curse, Adrian got very excited. She was already on the edge.

"Adrian? Remember what you said before?" Margaret whined softly. "That we could go away? We're going away from here, right?"

"Sure, baby," Adrian jerked off on top of her. "Right after you fuck me good."

"No!" Margaret cried, not wanting to lose her only friend. She tried to toss off her girlfriend.

Adrian was pleased with her struggle. The jostling about only served to make her more excited. She bit her girl-friend's leg as the model squirmed beneath her. "Where you goin'," she joked. "Huh?"

"Berlin. We're going to Berlin. Right?" Margaret pleaded. What will I do without Adrian? She thought, pan-icked.

"Why don't you good people hold her down for me so I can fuck her?" Adrian suggested gleefully. I am having a really good time, she noted to herself. When her audience seemed unwilling to participate, she informed them, "She likes it really, it's okay."

At first they weren't sure. But the assistants were used to doing what they were told, and the group around them seemed amused, so they helped Adrian out. They knew it was a favor they could get paid back for later. Adrian would remember.

"That's good," Adrian said, her struggling girlfriend held down like a sacrifice. "That's good," she said, moving delicately on Margaret's softest parts. "That's good," she said, gnawing on her muscled calf. "Adrian, you'll die," Margaret called out. "Good. Kill me, baby," Adrian answered. "No! NO! Stop!" Margaret called as Adrian's cry overlapped hers. "Yeeeeeaaaasssss."

Margaret didn't see her girlfriend disappear. She didn't want to witness another death. She heard their gasp of surprise and the quiet that comes after. Suddenly her hands were free. She curled up on the far wall and stared at the neon sign. She listened to it hum. I've got no one left, she thought, except the alien. I'm unnatural. A killer. A weirdo like him. An outsider. Nothing matters anymore. Then she felt free. Released like a bird. It doesn't matter what I do. I'm not like them anyway. I'm a creature like the alien, she decided happily. What I was before doesn't matter, it's just for the history books. She rose to her knees and looked around her. They were still staring quietly. Then she caught the eye of the redheaded one that Adrian had liked so much before. She wanted to know all about her then. I'll tell her now, she decided. It doesn't matter to me if she knows anymore.

"What have we done?" whispered the nervous stylist who had held Margaret down. Her assistant answered, "Wait a minute. If we think clearly, this can all be explained."

"It's easy to explain," Margaret called out to the whispering women. "You wanted to know who and what I am? I'm a killer," Margaret announced, enjoying her freedom. "I kill with my cunt. You can write about it in *Midnight Magazine!*" she said, laughing, and pulled the live wires of the sputtering neon sign. "Or *National Enquirer,*" she cried happily, seizing another group of wires from another electric sign. "It's going to be the new sensation!" she said grandly, as though doing a commercial. Margaret got off the bed and quickly pulled out all the wires of every neon sign. She wasn't frightened by the spitting wires. The others watched her bizarre behavior, not sure what to do. She knocked over the umbrella light and happily plunked in her makeup chair. The light fell to the ground enveloping her listeners in darkness. Margaret looked into the mirror. "I'm from Connecticut, '*Mayflower* stock,'" she said, staring at herself. "I was taught that my prince would come. And he would be a lawyer and I would have his children. And on the weekends we would barbecue. And all the other princes with their princesses would come and say 'Delicious, delicious.' Oh, how boring!" She reached to the single light still working in the apartment and turned it off. It had been illuminating her face.

Margaret dipped a sponge into a white, glowing paint upon her vanity. She spread the fluorescent film over her face, and suddenly they could make out her ghostlike features in the darkness. "And I was taught," she continued, "that I should come to New York and become an 'independent' woman. I would be an actress. And my prince would come and he would be an agent." On the word, she dipped her finger into another vivid color of fluorescent paint, and smeared a line on her face with it. She continued talking and painting herself, the paint applied almost as an illustration that went with her story. "And he would get me a role," she continued, without losing the tempo of her confession. "And I would make my living waiting on tables in a restaurant. And I would wait till thirty, till forty, till fifty. And I was taught that to be an actress one should be fashionable. And to be fashionable is to be androgynous. And I am androgynous not less than David Bowie himself. And they call me beautiful. And I kill with my cunt. Isn't it fashionable? Come on, teach me! I'll take lessons; how to get into show business. Be nice to your professor, be nice to your audience, be nice to your agent: Be nice. Be nice. Smile. How to be a woman? Want them when they want you. So, how to be free and equal? Fuck women instead of men and you'll discover a whole kingdom of freedom. Men won't step on you anymore, women will. So who's next? Who's gonna teach me? Are you afraid? You're right! Because they're all dead. All my teachers."

She seemed a child for a moment. A child lost in the dark, who didn't know where her parents were. Then there was a quick transition and the voice of a hard woman broke the silence. "What time is it?" Margaret demanded.

The confused stylist who had held the model down checked her watch. "It's one o'clock," she answered, surprised by Margaret's behavior.

"Well?" Margaret demanded, as though they were all idiots. "We should go to the Club." She stated it as though it were the obvious course of action, and then she dropped her dress. "There's nothing else to do," Margaret said, as she changed in front of the crowd. "We might as well dance. Let's go! Let's go!" she ordered, trying to get the group out of her apartment. They watched her get ready for the evening, still unsure what action to take. She seemed completely in control, even after all she had been through. And she looked fabulous. The perfect candidate for Club life. A black mask held back her hair like a hood, bleached blond strands sprouting from the eye and nose holes. Her makeup was strong, a primitive fluorescent mask. The red dress she wore had hanging black panels that offset her red legs to advantage. "Let's go!" she insisted. "Let's go!" she commanded, and ran out the door. Confused, the crowd followed her out of the apartment and into the elevator.

An eerie silence fills the long ride to the street in the darkened cubicle. Alternately, the riders look at Margaret's back—the ghoulish mask she wears as a hood stares back at them—and at each other. Each waits for the other to say something, but no one knows what to say. Having had participated in the public humiliation of their hostess, they all have a guilty glide down to the street.

The stragglers watch as Margaret hails the only visible cab. As they struggle with their equipment they watch her ride away, leaving them all stranded in the deserted section of town.

Scab Gets His

The first Club Margaret tried was a fast job. She could see the whole public area from one vantage point. She scanned the Club quickly, like an animal, and left without speaking to anyone. The people who knew her didn't find it unusual. It was fairly routine behavior.

It was at the second Club that she realized the object of her search might not be frequenting *her* haunts. As she climbed the dark stairs to the third floor the thought struck her. Abruptly, Margaret turned and pushed her way back down the single-file narrow staircase. It was aggressive, but that was common Club behavior for a regular. Most waiting to go up the stairs knew who she was.

As she pushed her way out of the Club, Jimmy approached her. A few of the fashion-shoot participants had come to this haunt. From where he had been lying on the wall, Jimmy had watched Margaret from when she had first entered the Club. He had watched her scan the dance floor, wanting to speak to her but not wanting the others from the fashion shoot to see. Now, as Margaret pushed her way to the door, the bad boy approached and asked a question timidly. He regretted what had happened, especially since it looked like Adrian was going to split, to break up with Margaret because of it. "Are you looking for Adrian?" Jimmy asked gently.

"Adrian is dead," Margaret answered, without even looking at the person. "It's every man for himself."

She left the Club, pushing her way into the street. The air was cool and wet on her face, but she wasn't chilled. Walking in long, even strides, Margaret headed toward another club, a club she wouldn't normally frequent. Having walked half the distance already, Margaret caught a cab, and within moments was deposited at the entrance to the large disco. The line was long with people who would never think to go to her club, but doormen are a special breed. This one recognized her from when he worked at another club. Margaret passed the portal without paying and walked the large entrance ramp to the disco.

As an animal stalking its prey, Margaret went into the forest of pulsating bodies after him. She careened across the dance floor, bumping into active dancers. The music was so loud it vibrated in their chests. Covering the space without success, she looked up to the second landing to continue her search. And then she saw him.

He was standing with the other "guys" who were watching girls move to the music. She laughed with glee when she saw the familiar face, Bingo, she said to herself, knowing he would be hers. Elated, she quickly made her way to the stairs.

At first Vincent didn't recognize the weird person in heavy makeup flying through the crowd toward him. Then, as she got closer, he saw the familiar brightly clad legs with platform shoes. He tried to move away, but with the momentum of her approach, she reached him before he could press through the sweaty crowd. Vincent fully expected her to strike him, and shied away from the punk model, trying to protect his face. Her open-mouthed laughter took him completely by surprise.

"I'm delighted to see you," she said rapidly. "You don't know how it thrills me."

It took him a moment to absorb what she was saying. "You're glad?" Vincent answered cautiously, slowly letting his arms fall away from his face.

"Sure I am, baby," Margaret said automatically. "You're the man." Quickly she pushed her hands into the opening of his brightly colored shirt. "I love your sexy body," she said, stroking his chest.

It was all too much for him to grasp. "You're freaky," he answered with an uncomfortable laugh.

"Sure I am, baby," Margaret said professionally. "Freaky for you." She knew what they liked to hear. "Let's go to my place," she said quickly. It was an offer he couldn't refuse.

It bothered him that she was so distracted as they rode in the taxicab to her apartment. If she was so hot for him, why didn't she talk to him, or touch him or something? he wondered. Margaret seemed to him to be in another world.

"Now that we've had drinks and dinner and coffee and brandy," Sylvia said, slurring, "wouldn't you like to make yourself more comfortable?" She was finding it difficult to get to the stoic stranger. Her inability to get him hot was making her irritable.

"I think it's time for me to update my notes," the scientist said, gently moving away from his drunken date. He felt guilty for bringing it up, but his duty was pressing on him.

"You are absolutely right," Sylvia agreed, not hiding her sarcasm. "Now is *the* perfect time." She rose quickly and moved to the window before him. Plopping into his positioned chair, she drunkenly mimed focusing the delicate telescopic instrument.

As soon as they entered the apartment, Margaret began undressing. He found her behavior upsetting. They hadn't spoken to one another since their meeting at the Club. As the pieces of her clothing were stripped away, revealing her skin, Vincent wondered if it was possible that the model was deranged.

Johann knew the drunken woman was provoking him deliberately. But he couldn't help falling into her rebuke and returning her anger. He became irritated. After all, he had work to do. She was fiddling with his machine like it was some kind of toy, and she didn't even know how to use it properly. When she finally got it focused, she sat and stared through the lens as if transfixed, and didn't even offer him news of what was going on, or offer to let him see.

Sylvia was unaware of Johann's anger. Through the telescope she was watching Margaret disrobe in front of yet another man, a new man. Some girls have all the luck, she said bitterly to herself as she watched the encounter unfold. She immediately became aroused, fondly remembering her last experience at the window. "Orgasms?" she said, surprising Johann. "Wasn't that the subject that we were dishh-cussing?"

It brought up a lot of fond memories for Johann, this drunken persistence. He felt compassionate toward the woman. She reminded him of his own dear mother. "Right now, I think I should study this alien," he said kindly.

This guy is really slow, thought Sylvia, exasperated. I'll

have to spell it out for him. "Do aliens have orgasms?" she slurred.

Innocently Johann replied, "They don't even have bodies."

Sylvia stood and flirtatiously walked around the large man. He could smell the alcohol on her breath as she passed close by him. "You are an alien in this country and I wouldn't exactly complain about your body." Getting no reaction, Sylvia thought, I know, if I let him watch he'll get excited! In a slovenly manner she indicated the vacant seat. "Be my guest," she reminded him.

Johann eagerly sat in the available chair and gathered himself for his work. Before he could even bring the lens to his eye, Sylvia deposited her body in the seat as well, sitting right in his large lap. Her hand rested on the telescope lens, just out of his reach. He couldn't even grasp it to look!

"Being a German alien, and a scientist, what do you think about German alien orgasms?" Sylvia drunkenly demanded.

Vincent was ready to depart. He felt cheated; she had promised him a good time and now he was sure that she was not even aware of his presence. Suddenly the inattentive, unclothed model turned and looked into his eyes. "This is going to be the fuck of your lifetime," she promised. Her breath kissed his skin.

"I have some coke," Vincent replied guiltily. He wanted to make up for the last time. He had promised to get her high before, and had never produced the goods.

Margaret authoritatively grabbed the belt of his pants and unzipped him. "I don't care about that," she said huskily, opening his belt buckle. "I just want you, now."

"You don't want any?" he said, astounded. He had thought she was a coke whore.

Greedily Margaret pushed him back on the bed. She

pounced over his body. Suddenly Vincent was aware of the wave of heat coming off her large frame. Lasciviously he looked at her breasts and long torso. So what if she's flipped, he thought gratefully, she's still a real good-looking piece. He started to stiffen. The aggressive actor prepared to push his penis into her hot hole. Before he could place his hands on her buttocks, Margaret's muscles closed over him. She's good, he thought as she massaged his member inside of her. Rapidly he swelled to his fullest size.

Her subtle muscular movements brought him close very quickly. "That's too good," he warned her. "What's your hurry?" he said seductively, smiling at her.

"I just want to please you," she replied. She was moving her pelvis in a circular motion, her body only touching his where she sat on him. This way, he could easily view her body and fluid movements. Vincent noticed her glassy eyes, and wild expression. "Do you want to hit me?" she offered.

"You're sick," he answered gleefully as she fluctuated his phallus.

"I've got so many problems with my brain it's a real pain in the ass," she answered. On the word "ass," she came down on him in a strong, clean stroke. She pulled back slowly and came down on him again in the same way. "No," said Vincent. "Stop!" he said breathlessly. "I'm going to come!"

Margaret knew she had him now. "Good," she answered, and began pumping on him with full fury. "Give it to me," she coaxed. "Fuck me. Give it to me," she said breathlessly. This creep is going to die, she thought, excited. The alien is going to kill him. Kill him dead. The thought made her wild. She became crazy. She wanted to suck the juice out of him, suck the life out of him. She saw the arrow fly into his scalp. The sliver of glass pierced his brain and she came.

Kill him, she said silently to her alien, her protector. Kill this fucker dead. In her pleasure she floated up. My mind is leaving my body, she thought happily. She felt her soul lifted out of her body and into the alien craft. It was bright with colors and warm in the cozy space with his energy. She fused with the light of the stars. His colors burst on her, energizing her, thrilling her into ecstasy. Varying electronic streams of energy pierced her essence. She was joined with her alien. Joined with him in his craft on the roof. When her body drew her back to her cold frame, Margaret was disappointed. She had wanted to stay with him in his small ship. It was cozy there. Only then did she remember the mortal.

The body of her victim had disappeared. Her sad shape was sore, her muscles stiff. It hurt to move her limbs. She lay in the dark room, relaxing on the platform bed. Better not to have a body, she mused. Better to be like the alien.

"Suppose orgasms are killing people," Sylvia persisted. "What would you say about a person who has multiple orgasms?" she provoked, trying to entice the large man.

The last thing Johann was interested in was intercourse with a woman who smelled like his dear, sweet, alcoholic mother. "I would say this person is real sexy," he answered plainly, his mind on other matters. He wanted to get back to his research. She must know that I would rather be watching than discussing trivial matters with her, he thought.

"And would you be interested in studying such a person? Being a scientist . . . and a German alien?" Sylvia slurred. Premeditatively Sylvia swung the lens to the man's large eye, so he could get aroused as well, watching the sexual activity there.

As Johann eagerly looked through the lens, he witnessed the death of Vincent. The glass arrow pierced his head, searing his brain, and killing the boy. Then his body crumpled into foil ashes and disappeared. How can I allow this to happen and not do anything? the man asked himself. What had been fine in theory he found disturbing in practice. I cannot stand passively by and let more deaths occur, he thought. A scientist is a doctor. A scientist is a healer. I am a scientist, Johann thought gravely. I have a duty to my subject.

"I'm sorry," he announced to the waiting woman. "I cannot stay." He stood, lifting the surprised Sylvia, and depositing her in the seat. "She is in great danger," he informed his hostess, and ran out of the apartment.

"Shit," said Sylvia after she heard the front door close. Stunned and disappointed, she didn't move for a while. Her spirit was deflated. Then she noticed the telescope. Of course, she thought, I can watch him through the window. Adjusting the lens, Sylvia saw the naked girl on the bed. Knowing my luck, she said to herself, this punk girl will succeed where I failed.

Bride of the Night

Margaret laid still for so long, the warmth left her body. She knew she should put something on. From where she was lying on the bed, Margaret could see all the garments she owned displayed on the clothes rack. What dress shall I wear? she thought unenthusiastically. Then she saw her long white one. Margaret remembered the dress that one of her relatives had given her so long ago. For your wedding, dear, the woman had said, pressing it preciously into her chest. Now I don't need it, thought Margaret happily. Because my sweetheart has no body. But he can still see you, a voice in her head reminded her. Probably he won't know what a wedding dress is, she thought, planning her meeting with him. But the dress is beautiful, the only real beautiful thing I have. She quickly rose and slipped the long lace dress over her form. It was a magical moment for her. She was going to offer herself to him, to her alien. Margaret hadn't expected to be so moved. The spirit of other women is on this dress, she thought, trying to explain her own sentimental reaction. Women have worn this dress before, when they joined in spirit with their lovers. For all time, she said to herself. For all time.

As she moved toward the door to the roof Margaret trembled. Why should I be frightened? she thought, surprised at her own behavior. She paused near the makeup table. I should be happy, not scared. Of all the girls on the planet, this alien picked me. Then she heard the noise in the hall. Instinctively, the girl scrambled for the nearby knife. No one's going to abuse me ever again, she thought warily. Then she realized, It's that damn scientist! and she hid the weapon behind her back as he dipped his head to enter the doorway.

He entered the dark apartment tentatively, his eyes unadjusted to the lack of light. "What do you want?" Margaret called out demandingly. He stood in the shadows, his face obscured by the darkness. Margaret was reminded of the tale of the Golem. As the large man moved toward her, Margaret thought, He's so big. And he even moves like a Golem. And she squeezed the hidden knife for security.

"My name is Johann Hoffmann. I am a scientist," he said softly, his voice thick with the German accent. Still, Margaret couldn't make out his features. Haltingly he continued. "I've come to get you out of here."

"What do you know?" a confused Margaret asked in an unfriendly manner. She was upset that her meeting with the alien would be delayed by this awkward giant. What is it he is trying to save me from? she wondered, in spite of her haste.

"I watched you through your window. I've witnessed the

deaths from over there," he informed her, pointing to the building across the way. "I know how and why they died."

"So, you tell me why they died," answered Margaret sarcastically. I'm living all this and a giant comes from the outside to explain to me? I'm wasting time, time that I could be spending with the alien, she thought crossly.

"What difference does it make to you now? Come with me," the scientist pressed her urgently. This girl doesn't realize that she's in danger, he thought, frustrated. She doesn't believe what I say, just like the other punk, the small one.

If he knows what I know, thought a confused Margaret, why does he find it dangerous for me? Didn't he see the alien kill the others to protect me? "Wait a minute," she answered him, aggravated. "You come into my place, and you want me to leave, but you don't want to tell me why?"

"Okay!" he answered impatiently. "You have a creature, an alien creature, on your roof." Yes. Yes I do! Margaret thought triumphantly. She had never really seen the evidence, but she had known. Known he was there. If the scientist can see him, I can see him, she thought excitedly. "Where?" she said, thinking, This scientist can show me precisely where the alien's ship is. Even though I've been inside, I've never seen its exact position. Quickly she moved to the roof, leading the scientist outside, only to be stopped by the lumbering giant's large, cool hand on her shoulder. "I study these creatures. You are in great danger," the scientist said. "Come with me."

This ghoul really can't expect me to leave with him now, when I'm so close, Margaret thinks, incredulous. "Tell me where he is," she insists.

His large hands closed over the rounded ends of her shoulders. He pushed her down; she felt weighted to the spot, as though her feet were glued. "Do you want to die?"

the frustrated scientist asked the girl, exasperated. "My theory is," the scientist explained, "that these creatures, aliens, feed off people like we feed off other creatures. They need for sustenance a substance similar to opiates. Heroin is an opiate. So this one came here for it, only he found something better. That substance is produced in the brain during orgasm and is similar in chemical structure to opiates. It is killing to get this substance."

Margaret was reeling from his diatribe. This is not true, she insisted in her brain. The alien loves me. I know he loves me. "He didn't kill me, did he?" she protested provocatively. "Why didn't he kill me?" Margaret says with a sexy superiority. I'll fix this freak, she thinks protectively. If I don't, he'll alert people to the presence of the alien, and my lover will fly away.

"Did you have an orgasm?" the scientist inquired professionally.

"No," Margaret lies in a helpless voice. She knew what to do. Running out to the roof, she cries, "Where are you? Where are you?"

Of course, as she expected, the scientist follows her outside. I've tricked him! she thinks triumphantly.

"Over there!" he says to Margaret, pointing to the upper roof. As she spys the craft she thinks, He wants to expose you, but I'll stop him. Then she plunges the knife into the large man's back. Except for the initial penetration of the outer layer of skin, the knife sinks easily into the man. Slowly, the German giant collapses to the tar roof. Sylvia can see too, Margaret realizes, solemnly looking across the concrete canyon to the building opposite. Soon she will be here as well as the others.

By now Katherine has already got directions to this place from someone who knows Adrian at the Club, Margaret muses knowingly. It won't be long before she shows up here too. Margaret turns, looking up to the roof, and addresses her prince.

"I've killed them all," she announces proudly to her alien. "There's no one left." Margaret feels sexy. "We can be together now," she promises her soulmate seductively.

Horrified, Sylvia rushes out the door in her kimono. I hope I can find the building, she worries, wondering if an ambulance can save him. I have to find the building and apartment before I can call, she thinks, panicked. I don't even know the number of the house.

"Come out," calls Margaret. "Come to me. If you want to feed on me, it's all right. I don't care. I want you to. Please come out. I know you care for me. I want to make love with you." Not knowing what response to expect, Margaret stares at the lip of the alien craft protruding over the edge of her roof. I wonder if he can see me? she thinks suddenly, staring into the pile of debris in which the craft is nestled. What do I do now? she wonders, confused. Suddenly, the small, shiny craft starts to rise. "No! No!" bleats a terrified Margaret. "You can't leave me now!" He knows the women are coming here to find their men and thinks he'll be discovered, she thinks, panicked. "Don't leave without me!" she screams. "Don't leave!"

I know what will stop him, she thinks, running back into the apartment. I know what he likes. Swiftly Margaret smashes the mask and pulls the packets of powder from the crumbling plaster. Into the bathroom she takes the stash; frantically she mixes the powder with water in a bent and battered spoon. Finally, she thought, all those years of watching this procedure have come to some use. Margaret could heat the mixture in the spoon adeptly. The bubbling potion is soon drawn into an abandoned syringe. She rushes from the bathroom rapidly, frightened that the craft has already departed. Pulling a sturdy leather belt from the clothes rack, Margaret runs out to the roof.

Here is some heroin for you, she thinks as she stares at the still-hovering craft. The heavy belt is looped around her white arm. For you, she thinks, as she pulls the belt tight on her biceps. Inserting the needle, she squishes the warm liquid into her bulging vein.

Katherine and Sylvia arrive from different directions, and each is surprised to see the other in Margaret's building entrance. They stare at each other oddly as they both enter the elevator. What would a woman like that be doing prowling around in this deserted building at this hour of the night? both women wonder.

The drug carries her away almost instantly and a wave of nausea follows. Why doesn't he take me? she wonders, frightened, as she sways in the night. Can't he see what I've done? Maybe I'm not close enough to him, she decides, navigating her way across the undulating tar surface. Precariously Margaret moves toward an iron ladder that leads to the upper roof. The black metal is rough and cool on her hand as she grasps it. Somehow it strengthens her resolve. This is real, she reminds herself, soothed by its rigidity. Holding the ladder, Margaret pulls herself onto the structure. Crawling up the vertical maze, fighting the effect of the drug, Margaret makes her way to her savior.

"Excuse me," says Sylvia swiftly to Katherine as she pushes the elevator buttons, "but I'm in a great rush. I have to go straight to the roof." She enters and pushes her floor button anxiously.

Instinctively, to Sylvia's chagrin, Katherine puts her arm into the closing elevator door's path. "The roof?" she asks. "Isn't that the same as the penthouse?"

"Yes," answers Sylvia impatiently as Katherine enters the

moving closet. He's probably dead by now, she thinks, aggravated, as she watches the elevator door finally close.

"Well," says Katherine, confused, "that's where I'm going." She's certainly rude, but this doesn't look like the type of woman who would go to a place where they sell drugs, Katherine thinks, frustrated. Maybe I have the wrong building. Although the description matches perfectly what that strange boy told me at the club. Katherine reconsiders. The music was loud, maybe I misunderstood. She stares at the nervous woman in the kimono. "I guess Adrian is having a party?" Katherine probes.

"Adrian?" Sylvia says hostilely. She must know these freaks, she thinks of the well-dressed woman. "Who's Adrian?"

Often Margaret would find herself stalled on the ladder, frozen in a precarious position. Sometimes her foot slipped on the satin of the dress. Its long, heavy, shiny train spilled down many rungs to the black tar surface she had left. It had stopped occurring to her to be frightened, however; she felt great, all-powerful, certain of her own importance. Margaret knew she could do anything, anything she wanted. This is a fabulous drug, she thought, euphoric. No wonder the alien likes it. But Margaret had no sense of time. She couldn't know that it was taking her a long while to make her way up the perfectly perpendicular structure.

When the elevator opened, both women looked at each other in surprise. They were not in an apartment, but on the nineteenth floor of the office building. "Where's the roof?!" said Sylvia, panicked. "This isn't the roof."

"This is as far as the elevator goes," responded Katherine, as she moved out of the elevator to search the hall.

"There must be stairs," decided Sylvia.

"Here's a sign!" Katherine cried, finding an open door to

the stairway. *Penthouse,* read the sign above the steep cement stairs.

Margaret pulled herself over the edge of the tar roof, squinting to focus her eyes on the hovering craft. At first she couldn't see it floating in the night. She stared into the black, struggling to her feet, worrying that it wasn't there. Eventually she saw the small, hovering object glow in recognition of her. Margaret stepped toward the edge of the highest roof where it hovered. As she trudged toward it, the alien seemed farther and farther away from her. Finally, the blue light escaping from the floating metal disk felt cool on her face, and she was standing before him. I am full of what you like, she thought, sure that he could read her every thought. I have a lot of heroin in me. Take me, she pleaded, offering herself to him.

The two women burst onto the roof. Sylvia examined the carcass of the scientist briefly, and then heard Katherine gasp. Looking up at Margaret, Sylvia caught sight of the girl jerking supernaturally on the upper roof. Bands of energy wrapped her dancing body and she was lifted and pulled like a puppet. He loves me! He loves me! Margaret thought joyously as she danced on the precipice. They see me in my dress, she thought happily. Those women are my bridesmaids. That's why they are here, she thought, feeling everything was right in the world. They are here to witness our union. The projection of electrons entered her body in a wave, small particles seeking the opiate juice. The wave consolidated into a long, flexible lance, which pushed into her chest, seizing her heart. He's taking me! Margaret thought, elated, as she joined with the energy. She felt her body being lifted, lifted and twisted, and Margaret was in ecstasy. It was so exciting, beyond what she had previously imagined. I wish it could have always been like this, she thought, as her body involuntarily spasmed with what she thought was pleasure. At the last moment, Margaret looked down at the women below. Their two sets of eyes looked on in horror as the quivering, flexing body of Margaret was sucked into the small craft and flown away.

It was the stench of the corpse rotting in the sun that brought the policemen to investigate. People in the building had started to complain. The patrolmen found the problem, then called in the precinct detectives.

They wouldn't even have noticed the second body, if the tail of train of the ornate dress the second victim was wearing hadn't flickered in the wind. It caught the eye of one of the police officers who had radioed in the call. The nauseated young patrolman had wandered away from the cardboard carton containing the rotting nude body of the male, and then caught sight of the bleached blonde. He called out, and as they examined her body, he took a reflective moment and really looked at the girl. He thought, It's sad that she died. She seems like someone I could like. She must have been sexy.

The official report assumed a lot. They couldn't locate the alleged roommate, and couldn't get a last name on her. The story they pieced together was that the older gentleman had had a heart attack during intercourse with the female, and the female had killed herself out of grief. There were no other tracks on the body than the fresh one from the incident. The other sperm in the female could not be explained. Neither could the apparent ability of the novice to shoot herself up be fully resolved. Finally, a surname for the girlfriend-roommate was uncovered, but, allegedly she had left the country and she couldn't be located. No one had claimed the body of either person by the time the report was filed. Overall, no one believed there was any actual criminal intent or involvement. So the investigation was discontinued for more pressing matters.